Special thanks to the friends who helped critique, edit, and inspire me to stay the course...

Ned Baker, Donna Bettinelli, Bill Falconer,

Miriana Kanzler, Harry Manko,

Susan Voorhees

And to my Editor-in-Chief

Lauren Bettinelli

I can't thank you enough for your considerable contribution of time and editorial expertise.

*

Please, however, forgive the occasional instances where I ignored the knowledgeable advice from all of you, and instead chose to use a good measure of poetic license. Sometimes, I just can't help myself.

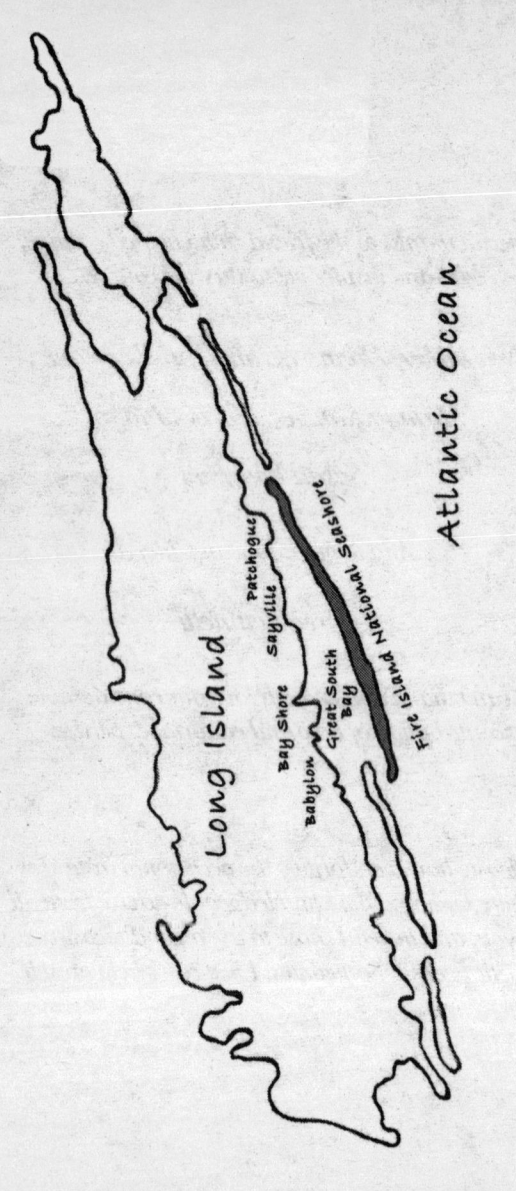

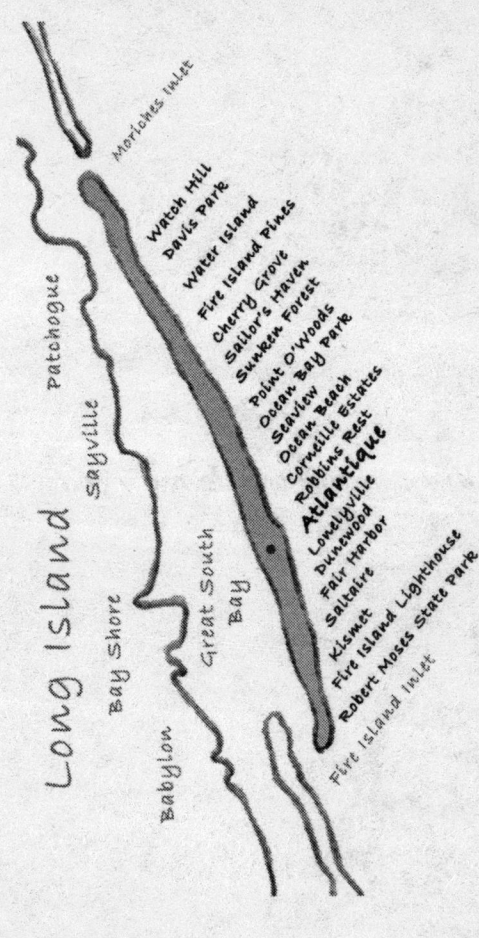

To Grace

My loving wife and dearest friend

Chapter 1

At first I'm thinking it's part of a dream, but as I sit up to gather my senses I hear the sharp rapping sound again. A quick glance at the clock tells me it's one thirty-five in the morning, and it takes but a split second for it to register that someone's boarded my boat with a strong desire to see me. The intensity of the knock and the time of night also make it pretty obvious this is not a social call. Terrible thoughts of a family emergency or a badly hurt friend begin to race through my mind. What other reason would motivate someone to intrude so urgently at this hour? My boat being on fire or sinking would have definitely qualified, but I think I was well positioned to be the first one to know of such awful news.

I grab the bathing suit I was wearing earlier in the day, and decide not to bother with a shirt. It's only a few steps out of the master stateroom, and then a dozen or so more to pass through the galley and across the salon. I see a vague silhouette against the darkly tinted glass of the door, cast by the lights that line the dock of the marina, but I'm unable to determine much in the way of an identity until I turn the lock and open it.

We formally met less than a dozen hours ago, and I'm not always good at remembering names, but this one I know by heart.

"Jill? Are you all right? What's the matter?"

She clearly takes those questions as an invitation to enter, and as she squeezes past me, she places her hand over the one I still have resting on the doorknob, pushing the door closed behind her. Even in the soft illumination of the cabin's courtesy lights it's easy to see how upset she is, and apparently about ready to cry.

"I'm so sorry to bother you Michael..." it comes out of her mouth as a loud whisper that's broken with emotion, and her tone suggests something close to hysteria, "but I have a bit of a problem and I don't know who else to turn to!" She now leans against me and starts to cry, her body is trembling.

This is quite a shock to say the least, and I'm not immediately sure what to do. After all, this woman is married, and I don't get the impression she's here on behalf of her husband. It also doesn't help matters much that he's a rather large fellow who is by all appearances insanely jealous. They've been coming here every weekend over the past month or so, but they are without a doubt newcomers this year. I'm sure of it. There's no way I would have forgotten this woman had I seen her before.

Not a man in this marina can manage anything less than a long glance in her direction when she makes her way down the dock... a knockdown gorgeous brunette, around five-foot-eight, dark blue eyes, and a figure that all too often entices me to daydream. Whenever I see those tantalizing breasts of hers bounce teasingly by, barely held in place by one of her sheer bikini tops, it's always the thought of heaven that comes to mind. Her hair looks soft and inviting, flowing most of the way down her slender back, and just below that, the perfect curves of her firm rear end and long silky smooth legs take over.

She carries herself in a way that suggests class and confidence rather than seeming full of herself, but she is no doubt aware of the considerable attention she commands. I constantly remind myself she's married though, and I'm careful not to stare too long, or let my tongue hang out of my mouth if I can help it. I do however at times get lost in thoughts of incredible passion when I'm watching her, and on more than one occasion I've earned a shot in the ribs from my girlfriend Allison in the process. Doing her best to painfully help me back to reality.

I realize I'm mentally drifting even now as I feel her leaning against me for comfort, and this stirs a sense of guilt. This is definitely not the time for that. I place my arm firmly around her, as my thoughts turn to her safety.

"Take it easy, I'm here. It's all right... What is it? Tell me what's wrong."

"It's that *bastard* I'm married to!" she half gasps, and then pauses only briefly to catch her breath. "He called me a few minutes ago from Ocean Beach. He's down there with some of his drinking buddies, half smashed as usual. He accused me of flirting with you earlier, and says he's going to punish me when he gets back to the boat."

"*Punish* you?" I'm sure the surprise is evident in my tone. "What does he mean by that?"

"Well, if it's anything like the last time, it means he plans to slap me around a little."

"*Slap you around?*" This whole scene is becoming unreal. "Are you *kidding me?*" Anger has now managed to substantially overtake my initial surprise. I'm far from being a saint when it comes to violence in general, but a man hitting a physically helpless woman is one thing that I find completely repulsive.

"I can't believe this! What kind of a lowlife degenerate are you married to?"

"Oh Michael, please, don't ever tell anyone I told you that. I'm so embarrassed, and I'm scared." She's genuinely pleading now, afraid she told me.

Her husband's name is Dave Preston, and the three of us introduced ourselves last afternoon as a result of Jill asking for a tour of my new boat. In my opinion they make for an odd looking couple, then again, looks aren't everything. My guess is he's pushing forty, which means he's got about five years on me, and I think a good ten on her. Standing at around six-two, he's close to two inches taller than me, but I weigh in at one ninety-eight and he's carrying at least seventy-five to a hundred pounds more than that. He's also quite bald with only a thin band of salt and pepper wrapped around the lower part of his large head, and the flab in his face seems proportionate to that of his stomach. All in all a fairly good looking guy in spite of the excess weight, but a striking contrast to her; and I therefore assumed he had other, more appealing qualities: like maybe one of the world's greatest lovers, or just a real sweetheart of a guy.

It was obvious he wasn't happy she had asked for the tour, and he not only insisted it be brief, but he hovered persistently close to her side the entire time they were on the boat. To be honest, I do remember her smiling pleasantly at me a number of times as we made our way around, but I chalked it up to nothing more than polite attention.

Her right arm has somehow found its way around my neck, which feels pretty good now that I realize it's there, and I sense that the right thing to do is hold her close.

"Don't worry, I won't tell a soul," I whisper into her ear, "but will you promise me that you won't continue to put up with that kind of crap? It's immoral. And what in the hell is he talking about, accusing you of flirting with me?"

I make it sound as if it's hard to believe such behavior from her is even remotely possible, but I'm finding myself hoping this lovely creature might confess she was guilty of something so exciting and daring; especially since I now know what kind of a moron she's married to. Unfortunately, she pushes away, and I realize that my questions have served to suddenly change her mood.

"It's too complicated to get into right now, and I think I've already told you more than I should have. All I really wanted to do was ask if I could borrow your couch until he gets back and falls asleep. Can you please just do that for me without asking me to promise anything in return?"

I guess I screwed that up royally.

"Of course. And I'm sorry, I certainly didn't mean to pry... but don't you think that under the circumstances, this might be the worst possible place you could stay?"

"It's okay, believe me. Once he gets over the initial surprise and anger of me not being there to rough up a little, he'll soon fall asleep. Then in the morning when he's sober, I'll scold him for being such a nasty drunk, and forcing me to sleep on the beach to avoid him. He'll feel guilty and apologize profusely, grope at my body and beg for forgiveness, promising he'll never do it again. And after that, we'll start the whole cycle of irrational jealousy all over again."

She pauses slightly, looking as if she's deciding where to go with this.

"Look Michael, I know we just met..." she places her right hand softly against my left cheek, looking up into my eyes. Her voice has become very tender, almost as if she sensed I was hoping for more, and wanted to sooth any wound she might have inflicted by pulling away so quickly. "But I have this sense about you that you're a decent man and someone I can trust. There's absolutely no one else around here I feel that way about, and I would rather not spend the next several hours alone on the beach if I can help it. Is that okay?"

The change in her tone and expression as she finishes makes it clear I've already provided all the emotional support she might have needed, and that she would very much appreciate being by herself at this point.

"Okay, no problem. You know where I'll be if you need anything, and you might find the bed in the guest cabin a lot more comfortable than the couch."

"Please. If it's all the same to you, I'm fine right here."

"Suit yourself, but at least let me get you a fresh set of sheets."

She offers no argument and smiles appreciatively as I go. I return shortly with some spare sheets and a pillow.

"This is very sweet of you Michael. Thanks."

"You're more than welcome. You know where everything is, so just make yourself at home."

"Okay I will. Thanks again, and good night," she whispers softly.

"Good night." I reply softly as well.

I quietly close my cabin door behind me, and prepare for what I know will be a restless attempt at sleep.

Chapter 2

It's only a few minutes after six when I conclude that the possibility of further sleep is out of the question. Thankfully I did manage to grab a few hours, but I've been tossing around for a while now and I'm finally unable to wait any longer. Not that I suspect there's any chance she's still on board, but I have to know for sure. Maybe it was all just a dream.

A check of the salon before I hit the head for my first morning ritual offers nothing less than expected. The sheets have been refolded nicely and stacked on the center of the couch. I find myself unable to suppress the urge to walk over and lift them to my face. I momentarily savor the lingering scent as I remember it from when she leaned against me last night. Well, so much for the dream theory. I pick up what appears to be a note lying on the table next to the couch and open it.

> *Dear Michael,*
> *I can't thank you enough for being the kind and decent man I thought you were.*
> *Love,*
> *Jill*

She might not feel that way if she knew what I was thinking every time I see her walking by in her bathing suit. And I suspect that it will now be even more difficult not to stare and wonder. I am, however, touched by the note, and her use of the word "love". I head back to my cabin to find a safe place to hide it. This is definitely a keeper.

Forcing myself mentally back to the reality of my normal life, which is certainly nothing to complain about, I complete my initial bathroom call and then start a pot of coffee. Back to the head while the coffee is brewing for a shave and brush of the teeth, and then I'm off to my perch on the flybridge where I always enjoy the first cup of the day.

It's a Saturday morning in the middle of June with the forecast calling for nothing less than scorching sunshine, and as I scan the marina I can see it was a good thing I came over here yesterday. With still about a week to go before the official start of summer, there's not a single slip left that's large enough for my boat. And, once the kids are out of school in a couple of weeks, even Friday afternoons will be chaotic: with people coming over as early in the day as possible, hoping to secure their spot for the weekend.

There are several medium sized slips still open, but my dear friend Vinny better get here in the next hour or two, or he'll be leaving his boat out on its anchor and wading his way to shore. I know from experience that a phone call to warn him is a waste of time. With or without it, he'll still get here when he gets here.

The name of this marina is Atlantique, and it's located on a thin strip of barrier beach called Fire Island. Fire Island runs parallel to the south shore of Long Island for more than thirty miles, sheltering a good part of it from the direct forces of the Atlantic Ocean, and almost the entire span is accessible only by boat. As the crow flies, Atlantique is pretty much due south of Bay Shore, which is where I live. But, to avoid the dangerous shallows of the Great South Bay, you have to follow the deeper water of the main channels, and do some zigzagging to get here. It's a town marina that accommodates around a hundred and fifty boats, providing nothing more than basic hookups of electricity and water. There's not much else to the place, other than a couple of playgrounds for the children, old plywood shower stalls that barely piss water, and a run down snack bar that's appeared ready for sudden collapse ever since I can remember.

Atlantique does, however, boast less than a five minute walk to a beautiful sandy ocean beach on the opposite side of the island, a beach that runs the entire length of the island, and in many places can only be accessed by a footworn path in the sand, or a narrow boardwalk winding through an abundance of dense thicket. In reality, you're only several miles away from the mainland, but the feeling you get is as if you're in another world, and I suppose that in many respects you really are. Town residents pay somewhere between twenty to thirty dollars a night to dock here on a first come, first served basis. The fee varies based on the size of your boat and on whether it's a weekday or weekend evening; but a better bargain than this, I would challenge you to find anywhere.

For me, there is something extremely special about being here, and for those of us who get this place in their blood, there is no substitution. People young and old, from just about every walk of life you can imagine, come in boats of every shape and size. Glancing around the marina this very second, I see boats that are probably worth no more than a couple of thousand bucks, and others that easily cost more than a million. I myself have graduated to bigger and more luxurious boats a number of times over the past ten years or so, with this latest one setting me back almost eight hundred grand. But like they say: you can't take it with you. And when there's something that you do that gives you this much pleasure, and you can afford it, it hardly seems excessive. I've always had a thing for Riviera yachts, and when I saw this new forty-two flybridge at the Miami Boat Show last year, I knew I had to have it. With two staterooms, two heads, a fully customized galley, and almost a fifteen-foot beam, I'm pretty sure it has more than enough room and amenities to thrill me for years to come. It's funny though, because it seems no matter how big of a boat you have, you're almost always thinking that something a little bigger might be better.

When my ex-wife Gina and I were first married, we used to spend an entire week here at a time, on an old twenty-four foot Sea Ray express cruiser. We barely had enough room to stand side by side in the cabin, much less store all of our stuff, and we had to convert the small dinette table into a bed every night. But we thought we were on top of the world when we first got that boat, and I remember thinking at the time that life couldn't get much better than that.

Looking out towards the sun now, as it breaks free of the horizon, I find myself smiling at the thought of Gina, which doesn't happen too often anymore. What a fool I was. So in love and trusting, I didn't realize she was having an affair right under my nose with the doctor she worked for. I was just starting a business and working ridiculous hours, and she insisted I allow her to help us afford the better things in life by working longer hours herself. Little did I know the kind of work she was being paid for after normal office hours.

It shattered my heart at first, but I got over the worst of it inside of a year. I came to accept that it had never been what I thought it was anyway, and that I simply had to move on. Besides, I had a growing business to run, and it certainly didn't spare me much time to sit around and cry over spilt milk. It seemed so unimportant to me at the time, but the silver lining in all of it was that she didn't want any part of the business or any other financial compensation in the settlement. She was so convinced he had more money than he knew what to do with, and that she was about to embark on a life of luxury I would never come close to achieving. To be totally fair, I do think she also felt a little genuine sorrow for me.

Knowing me as well as she did, though, she did make me promise that I wouldn't make any trouble. More specifically, she wanted my word that I wouldn't kick the shit out of Richard, or *Dick,* as I preferred to call him. But, I figured it took two to tango, and the thought of holding him personally responsible had never occurred to me. I was more than happy to just sign and get it over with.

The bitch of it all was, at least for her anyway, was that she didn't wind up being Dick's last fling, and he wasn't as well off as she thought. These days I know she's living back home with her parents, Vic and Mary, and I get the sense that things are financially strained. Vic calls me now and then, bitching about his hardware business being trampled by the larger chain stores, and he always makes it a point to let me know Gina's hoping I'll call her sometime. He has no idea how finished we are, and he doesn't understand why I won't call him dad anymore. It's kind of sad. I did think of him and Mary as my second parents there for a few years, but when something's over for me, it's over. I don't know how else to say it.

Down to the galley I go for my second cup of coffee, and I grab a boating magazine before I climb back to the bridge. I'm in a slip on the west side of the main basin's south dock, which runs along the shoreline. It's where most of the larger slips are grouped together. Looking out across the west dock, I see the Preston's thirty-four-foot Carver resting quietly in the calm water. I can't help but recall Jill's unpleasant anticipation of how Dave will grope for the pleasure of her body this morning; and try as I might, I'm unable to stop my mind from creating a picture of that ugly scenario, and the thought of it happening at this very moment.

I shiver my head and shoulders quickly, trying to jar the thought loose from within me, and I refocus myself towards the bay where an early morning freight boat is making its way across from Bay Shore. They're married, it's none of my business, and that's that. I'm here to enjoy myself.

Chapter 3

The Fire Island National Seashore begins at the Fire Island Inlet, which is formed, in part, by the tip of Robert Moses State Park, and continues all the way east to Moriches Bay, where the infamous Hamptons take over. Atlantique is located about a third of the way heading east from the inlet. A string of bridges provides access from the mainland to the parking fields of Robert Moses, but there are no paved roads for vehicles east of that. There are just a number of beach house communities with an assortment of walkways designed more for foot traffic, wagons, and bicycles. Some towns boast a small general market, a few even have a restaurant or two, and save for the absence of automobiles, the community of Ocean Beach resembles something close to a regular town. Some, however, have no commercial establishments or public facilities whatsoever.

If you're not a boat owner, the only way to get here is by taking a ferry out of Bay Shore for towns to the west, or out of Sayville or Patchogue for points east. Special freight ferries deliver all of the heavy goods, and most homeowners would be hard pressed hauling essentials without the help of their little red wagons. I think those rolling workhorses have even been designated as some sort of an official icon of the island.

I normally enjoy an early morning jog on the beach when I'm over here, and today was no exception. The first leg was about two miles up to the lighthouse, just shy of Robert Moses, and then I doubled back past Atlantique for better than a mile down to the rock jetty at Ocean Beach. With the tough part out of the way, I went into town and grabbed some fresh fruit and a newspaper at the market, and then I walked back along the ocean at a more relaxed pace, slowly taking in the beauty of the shoreline. The whole routine took about an hour and a half.

Vinny just called to tell me that he and the girls were approaching Crazy Charlie, which is the nickname for the flashing cross channel buoy not too far west of here, so they'll be here in a couple of minutes. It's coming up on ten o'clock and the timing worked out pretty well. I'm done showering, I put on a fresh bathing suit and T-shirt, and now I'm heading to the bow of my boat to watch them arrive and see where they dock. There are a couple of slips still open on the west dock, and that's likely what he'll opt for. We have a nice clambake and lobster fest planned for tonight, and while having our boats relatively close together isn't a necessity, it certainly makes things easier.

Vinny D'Angelo has been my best friend ever since we first met in junior high school. He's also now the vice president of my company and the only person to own stock in it other than myself. I trust and love him as much as I would my own brother, if I had one, and I know he feels the same way about me.

Joining me roughly three years after I started, he helped me considerably in building the business into what it is today, which is about fifteen million in sales and almost a hundred employees. It hasn't gone without financial reward either. You'd never know it by looking at him, but at the age of thirty-five he's already a millionaire a couple of times over, and that's not counting his twenty-five percent share of the company stock.

At six-foot-three, he's nothing less than two hundred and twenty-five pounds of solid muscle, with a dark European complexion that makes it look as if he's always got a tan. He likes to comb his jet-black wavy hair straight back around his ears, and he keeps his sideburns long and thin. They run towards his chin at the bottom, barely connected to the well-trimmed mustache that narrowly continues straight down from both sides of his mouth. He's a very handsome, tough looking guy, at least until he smiles that is. There's nothing quite like watching Vinny smile. He's got some of the whitest, most perfect teeth I've ever seen, and this huge smile that at times makes him look almost goofy because he's so damn happy.

Knowing him as I do, one of the most amazing things about him is that he still has any teeth at all, much less a mouth full. His father was a semi-pro boxer and he had Vinny boxing competitively before he reached the age of five. Martial arts training began before he was ten, and he's never taken a breather since. The only thing is, he must have missed class on the day they were teaching to use violence as a *last* resort, and when he gets mad at someone, they usually wind up in a lot of pain without much advanced notice.

A good fight was one thing we both got some sort of sick pleasure from as younger men, and during our formidable years we roughed it up with anyone that wanted to rumble. I was nothing close to being the fighter Vinny was, but I made up for a good measure of it with sheer determination. That was years ago though, and I try to avoid conflict now like the plague. I simply have too much to lose. And besides that, I don't heal so fast anymore. Vinny on the other hand hasn't changed all that much, and he worries me greatly at times.

More than being his best friend, Vinny also reveres me as the source of his financial good fortunes, and if you ever spend some time around us, it's easy to see the respect and appreciation that results from that. It's hard to explain, but although we're best friends of the same age, and truly consider each other as complete equals, he can't help but regard me as something of a *godfather* - his provider if you will. It's an Italian thing that I'm not totally comfortable with, but I do understand; and truth be known, I find it an honor to be thought of that way.

The reality of it is, I am the boss, and I ultimately call the shots. To his credit, Vinny understands that very well, and I can't remember even one occasion during all the years he's worked for me that he's ever attempted to take advantage of our friendship. Business is business, and he's always worked hard to earn everything he's gotten.

So that's me in nutshell I guess: Michael Hubbard, the WASP godfather. There are, however, a number of people who work for me that seem to feel the same as Vinny, and I figure that overall it means I must be doing something right.

There's the big lug now, slowing down as he approaches the No-Wake Zone at the mouth of the marina. Sure enough, he's aiming for the west dock. I turn and head aft along the starboard gunwale, stepping down into the cockpit...

"Hey, I never got a chance to ask you yesterday... are we talking potato or poker?"

Jill's standing there on the dock by herself, a long white cover-up hiding what I'm sure is a great looking bathing suit. The shirt declares her part of the *Atlantique Cocktail Team*.

Her smile is captivating.

"Are you okay?"

"Yeah, I'm fine," she offers without much enthusiasm, "everything went pretty much as expected... Did you get my note?"

"Yes I did, and it's already made its way into my scrap book."

She smiles again. "So what is it, potato or poker?"

She's pointing at my transom, and I realize she's referring to the name of my boat - *Chips*.

I smile now too. "Neither one. Try titanium and aluminum."

"What?"

"Titanium and aluminum. *Metal*. I'm in the machining business, and we machine solid blocks of metal into finished parts used to build airplanes. The metal shavings milled away from the solid block are referred to as chips," I wave my finger playfully in her direction, "and make no mistake about it, chips are a very valuable commodity."

She now points a finger playfully back at me as she grins and cocks her head slightly.

"*That* I can see."

Not only beautiful, but she's cute as a button.

"Which way are you heading?" I ask. "I have friends coming in on the west dock."

"Then that's where I'm heading. How about walking me to my boat?"

"You sure that's not going to be a problem?"

"Not for me. You're going that way anyhow, and after all, we were formally introduced yesterday. It's nothing more than a lucky coincidence we happened to bump into each other."

There goes that smile again, and there is trouble written all over it.

"Let's go then," I say, as I step onto the dock.

She's staring right at me. "You're the only person I've ever met that has eyes bluer than mine."

"Oh?" I ask innocently. "They're that noticeable? No one's ever told me that before." I smile at the lie.

"Yeah right. I almost believe that."

It takes us only a few seconds to reach the west corner of the south dock, and then we turn right heading north.

"I saw you leaving to run this morning. Can I ask where you go?"

"Oh, usually up to the lighthouse first, then down to Ocean Beach and back."

"That's a pretty good workout."

I see Vinny starting to back in, and it looks like he's going to be only two slips north of the Preston's; this ought to be nice and cozy.

"Yeah. But the way I tend to eat and drink over here, I've got to push myself a little."

"Well, for whatever my opinion's worth, I think you look great."

"Why thank you very much." It somehow sounded like something more than a friendly compliment, but I'm not about to go there. Dave is watching us approach from the cockpit of their boat, and Allison's standing in the cockpit of Vinny's, peering more than casually in this direction.

"Morning Dave," I say lightheartedly as I pass their boat and Jill breaks off to step aboard, "you two enjoy the day."

"Thanks Michael. You too," she replies, but I don't hear Dave say anything until I'm a good boat slip away.

"What were you doing with that jackass?" he questions her.

That comment I don't appreciate, and I'll make it a point to settle the score for that, the first chance I get. But for now I keep moving on my way. I reach the slip that Vinny's pulling into, and as I turn to watch his approach, I can still see the two of them in the corner of my eye, Dave now grabbing her by the arm.

"You're hurting me!" I barely hear her cry it out over the sound of Vinny's engines.

It's easy to see how quickly this guy resorts to violence, and I'm momentarily tempted to walk back over and get a little violent with him. But I see her wrestle her arm free, and after he looks around to see who might be watching, he doesn't attempt to grab it again. She appears to say something, and then enters the cabin alone, sliding the door closed behind her. He follows a few moments later, and I listen for the sound of a fight, but if anything further is being exchanged, I can't hear it.

I have this funny feeling that he and I will be getting to know each other a little better in the very near future, but right now is not the appropriate time. I focus my attention back on my buddy as he skillfully swings the stern of his boat between the pilings. He's concentrating directly aft on the corners of his transom until he's safely inside and then his focus shifts to me and I get one of those big smiles.

"Michael!" he shouts out excitedly.

I'm already getting *the look* from Allison as she hands me the starboard line first, and I decide to ignore her for now.

"Chenz!" I yell back affectionately.

I look down at the name on the transom and begin to chuckle. I'm still not used to it yet. The boat is a brand new Wellcraft 330 Coastal with a half tower. He has it rigged for deep-sea fishing, which is really more about image than something he'll ever do, and the name he settled on is *REEL HARD*.

"I can see it didn't take long for the two of you to become friends." Allison can't help herself.

"Good morning to you too, sweetheart," I reply cheerfully, and then I greet the other passenger left of Vinny - "Hi Debbie."

"Hi Michael."

Debbie Palazzo is Vinny's latest flavor, and I guess they've been together now for a couple of months. Nice Italian girl, but a bit heavy with the makeup for my taste. Vinny loves that stuff. She's a beautician in her late twenties, and stands about as tall as Jill, with curly brown hair that falls just below her shoulders. An attractive lady with relentless energy, and she's a lot of fun to be around.

Allison Wells has a more refined way about her. Standing a couple of inches shorter than Debbie and quite a bit thinner, she wears her dark brown hair short, always blown back neatly around her ears; but not so much that it hides her large diamond earrings, and I notice the right one sparkling brightly in the sunshine as she hands me the port line. I know she was hoping desperately for an engagement ring instead, but trust me, that is never going to happen.

She's fairly good looking with pretty green eyes, and she's not bad in the sack, but there's something about her that doesn't totally work for me. She's a well educated computer programmer that at times can be annoyingly stuffy, and I suppose that's the crux of the problem. She's pretty full of herself, and much too stiff for my taste on a permanent basis.

And as I think about it some more, strike the sack compliment, she's honestly not all that good. The sad reality is that my expectations just aren't as high as they used to be. I have Gina to thank for that. Oral sex in particular was something that my ex enjoyed with a passion, and the pleasure she could make me feel was unbelievable. We fed from each other so naturally, both wanting to make the other feel even more pleasure than we did ourselves. Slow teasing foreplay was almost always a given, and the climax was never anything less than intense exhilaration, a feeling of complete and absolute satisfaction. Unfortunately, no one has made me feel that way since.

Allison's approach to sex is more like following a procedure, and she prefers to go about it the conventional way. Well, at least that is when it comes to how I get my pleasure. She never complains if I want to go down on her first. Not that she won't try to *accommodate* me on special occasions, or if she wants something out of the ordinary, but even then, the experience is not nearly as great for me as she thinks it is. There is simply no substitute for genuine passion. With her noticeable desire to bring the event to closure as soon as possible, and a box of tissues always at the ready, she never manages to bring the word *thrilling* to mind.

Why even bother?

We met about a year ago by way of introduction through a mutual friend, and I'll be surprised if we make it through this summer. At thirty-three years of age, the idea of marriage is growing ever more heavy on her mind, and while I keep telling her it's not even close to being on my radar screen, (at least with her anyway), she doesn't seem to hear me.

She had to attend a friend's baby shower last night and was upset I wouldn't wait until this morning to bring the boat over with her on it. Oh well, life goes on. It amazes me that she doesn't understand the incredible pleasure I get from using the boat as much as possible, or the concern I had over potentially not getting a slip for the weekend.

With the stern lines set, Vinny cuts the engines and walks to the transom to shake my hand. To me, there's nothing like a good firm handshake.

"Long time, my friend," he grins a little.

"How was the bay? Looks pretty calm from here."

"Yeah, wasn't too bad. With the wind out of the south, it's a little snotty on the other side, but it's completely flat once you reach the channel running along West Island."

Allison reappears after grabbing her bag from down below, which she now hands to me.

"Thanks Vinny."

"You're welcome Allison." He looks over to me. "I assume we're planning on some beach time?"

I take Allison's hand as she steps up and onto the dock.

"I think that's the plan."

The girls both smile their agreement.

The two of them could sit on the beach yakking all day. Don't get me wrong, I love the beach too, but after no more than a couple of hours at best, I start to get a bit antsy and usually head back to the boat or take a walk into one of the neighboring towns.

I look at Vinny. "Why don't you settle in and swing by whenever you're ready. If we're not on the boat, we'll be at the beach."

"Sounds good to me... Oh, and in case I forget later, I've got the weekly Operating Report for you." He grabs a thick folded envelope from his back pocket and hands it to me. I stick it in mine.

"Thanks Chenz. See you in a few."

Allison and I walk quietly down the dock, canvas bag in my left hand, my right hand holding hers. Surprisingly, nothing more is mentioned at the moment in regard to Jill. I noticed the cabin curtains pulled shut as we passed the Preston's boat, but didn't hear a sound.

Allison also knows better than to question me about the odd looking Operating Report. That mistake she has already made once before.

There are certain perks in every business, and ours is chips. We sell some of it as a matter of record, and we sell the rest under the table. It's unreported income, and therefore illegal, but certainly not an unprecedented practice among principal owners of smaller shops in our industry. If anything, it's more of a tradition. We average about two grand of extra cash each week between us, and it's nice pocket money. Vinny gets his twenty-five percent, and the rest is mine. It's not the kind of thing you ever discuss with anybody else.

I bring Allison's bag to my cabin, and stash the "report" while I'm there. After that, we decide not to wait, and head for the beach.

Chapter 4

It's a straight walk south from the main basin of the marina to the ocean, past an old handball court, a second set of showers and then the snack bar. Once past the snack bar, the cement walkway inclines gradually for several hundred feet as you approach the top of the dunes, the smell and sound of the ocean coming up to greet you before you see it. Then it's just a few wooden steps leading down to the sand.

The tide is out right now and the ocean is rather calm. There's already dozens of blankets making their claim to choice spots of soft sandy real estate. We trod around them with beach chairs and umbrella in hand, staying left of the lifeguard stand and crossing about halfway to the surf line. The beach took a pounding over the winter, leaving much less sand than we had last summer. It presently extends no more than maybe a hundred yards from where the steps meet the sand, and that's at low tide. A couple of more nasty storms this year, and there's a good chance the ocean will broach some of the narrowest points of this tiny island just as it did around ten years ago.

The morning sun is already strong enough to burn those of us with lighter skin, and by the time one o'clock rolls around, the sand nearer the dunes will be so hot that even the strong of heart will need sandals to tackle it. But the soft breeze that blows across the cool ocean water tends to balance things out nicely, and that's what makes being near the sea so wonderfully pleasant most of the time. I always wear some sort of hat to protect my face from the sun, and if I plan on being here for more than an hour or so, I bring an umbrella to shelter the rest of me. Allison puts on nothing more than a little sunscreen and sits directly in the sun most of the day, not being phased in the least. Vinny's no different than Allison, and Debbie comes in a close second, wearing only a hat most of the time.

Allison remains uncharacteristically quiet, and I'm beginning to think something serious is up. She wasted no time once we got here, wandering over to a large cache of seashells without inviting me; I'm sure to look for beach glass. We usually look together, and we've accumulated a dishful of the colorful stuff over the past year that we keep on a shelf in the salon.

A sudden blast of the lifeguard's whistle interrupts the more subdued background noise of people talking and children playing: the shrill of it lingering in the warm gentle air for a few seconds, then beginning to blend more nicely with the other sounds of the beach as it drifts slowly away.

Well, whatever her problem is, I'm sure I'll hear about it soon enough. But for now I'm enjoying the solitude, and I turn my attention to the newspaper I brought along.

It's getting close to eleven o'clock before I see Vinny appear at the top of the steps, trying to get a read on where we are. There are two ferries that bring day-trippers to Atlantique from the Bay Shore Marina. One leaves Bay Shore at ten in the morning, and the other at noon. It takes them roughly forty minutes to get here on average, and it's something worth keeping in mind if you're choosey about where you sit on the beach or if you're planning on having lunch at the snack bar. On any given day, the crowd that arrives can easily strain the resources of both facilities. Vinny doesn't concern himself with such trivial things as ferry schedules, and loves to break my chops because I do.

I can see the look of utter disgust on his face from here, a chubby kid about a third of his size standing behind him with a boogie board, trying to push him down the steps and out of his way. Another one close by is screaming at his mother for not stopping at the snack bar for ice cream. I somehow can't help myself, and I wait to call out to him, enjoying the view of well-deserved misery as the crowd pushing past him continues to grow.

I do, on the other hand, begin to feel sorry for Debbie.

"Hey Chenz! Over here!" I hold up my arm.

His face brightens immediately, and down the steps he comes. Navigating clear of several families, he makes his way across the sand, a beach chair clenched in each hand and a bag on his shoulder.

"What's up with the sudden crowd?" I ask innocently as he nears, and then I'm unable to suppress a grin.

He now realizes I was enjoying myself at his expense.

"Crowd?" He looks back over his right shoulder for effect. "Gee, I didn't even notice."

He breaks into a silly looking grin of his own as he turns back to me, and I can't hold back a laugh. I take the chair from his left hand and wrap my right arm around his shoulder, pulling myself close to him.

"Tough little kids, huh?" I laugh again.

"You two are too much," Debbie scolds us nicely. "Where's Allison?"

I nod my head towards the surf. "Looking for beach glass."

She heads over to join her as Vinny and I set the chairs in place. We sit down only a few feet apart, angled slightly toward one another but mostly towards the water. I glance slowly up and down along the shoreline, taking in the beauty of it all, and then finally over to Vinny.

"Did I miss anything exciting yesterday afternoon?"

"Not really. Sales remain on target and we received the payment we were hoping to get from International Aerospace."

"What a great company to work for. One of the very few that regularly pays their bills early."

"Yeah, that's for sure. And hey, speaking of people paying their bills on time, Fat Tony called looking for another favor. He has a couple of parts he's in trouble on and he needs twelve pieces of each in three weeks."

Anthony Russo, or Fat Tony as we like to refer to him more affectionately, is a cousin of Vinny's on his mother's side. Almost twenty years older than Vinny, he's a third-generation owner of a company in the same type of machining business we are, around triple our size. Born with a silver spoon in his mouth, he has never had to break a real sweat in his entire life, his father made sure of that. His physique is similar to that of Dave Preston's, but the flab in his case far outweighs the muscle. If he ever does find himself in need of some real muscle, he definitely pays for it.

Now you would think that someone as fortunate as that would be downright grateful and somewhat humble, diligently working to preserve the legacy his father and grandfather worked so hard to create. But Fat Tony is anything but humble, and he has little respect for anyone, especially the people that work for him.

I know this for a fact too, because Vinny and I both worked for him when we first got out of trade school, and the experience was so lousy it wound up being the motivation I needed to break out on my own. Thank God. If Fat Tony hadn't been such a prick, there's a good chance I'd still be working for him, struggling to maintain something close to a middle class standard of living.

I'm sure to this day he also resents the hell out of the fact that Vinny has done so well by leaving him to join me, but as we both often say… Fuck him. With three divorces already under his belt, and marriage number four looking more doubtful with each passing week, the man is a financial disaster well in the making. He sucks every dime he can out of the business and blames everyone other than himself for all of his problems.

"Is Engineering cleaned up to the point where they can handle the work?"

"Yeah. I might have to pitch in a little myself, but we'll get it done if you give me the word."

"What did you tell him?"

"I said I thought it might be possible, but I had to run it by you. I also told him that he still owes us a hundred and fifty grand from the last favor we did, and that it's now over a hundred and twenty days past due."

"Good. What did he say?"

"He laughed like he always does, acting like he was offended I even brought it up. Telling me how grateful we should be for his business, and that we should know by now he's good for it sooner or later."

"What an asshole… Okay…"

I find myself needing to stand as my anger begins to stir, and then I turn, pointing down momentarily at Vinny. "Call him on Monday and tell him no problem... Make sure you're comfortable with the tooling estimate out of Engineering, and then add twenty grand for good measure. Then you wait until we're ready to make delivery, and we have a hold of him good and firm by the short hairs. If his last bill isn't paid by then, I want *fucking* C.O.D. for everything before he gets a single lousy part... and this time, Vinny, I'm not screwing around."

I settle back down in my chair, and then lean towards him as I continue. "And you know what else, even if he does pay in full before then, which I seriously doubt he will, I want fifty percent of the new work C.O.D. At least we'll recover all of our direct costs and a good portion of the overhead expenses without waiting another four or five months for the privilege."

He shakes his head in thoughtful agreement. "Okay... done. And I like it. It's about time we taught that disrespectful son of a bitch a lesson. Don't worry, I'll take care of everything... personally."

"Good."

We sit silently for a minute or so, the sound of the ocean gradually calming me down.

"Hey, you'll never guess who spent some time on my boat last night."

He looks over at me, at first without a clue. I smile slightly as I nod my head, my expression encouraging him to think the unthinkable.

It becomes more obvious after we exchange a few glances, and now he starts to smile too.

"No way. Are you yanking my chain?"

I keep nodding my head in the affirmative.

"Get out of here!" he's clearly surprised and impressed, but keeps the volume of his voice within reason.

"You sneaky son of bitch! How did you pull that off?"

"I didn't, she just showed up. And believe me, nothing happened."

"Nothing? Come on. You've never been that innocent in your entire life. Then why did she drop by?"

"Her husband's a nasty drunk, and she was afraid he was going to beat her up when he got back from drinking with the boys down at Ocean Beach. All she wanted was somewhere to hide out until he got back and fell asleep. Can you believe that?"

He takes on a more serious look. "The world can be a lousy place sometimes Michael, you know that. And much worse things are going on around us all the time."

The girls are heading back to join us, and we change the subject back to Fat Tony. Vinny's heard a rumor that he's close to filing for bankruptcy. I know rumors are often cruel and undeserving, but it's all the more reason we should get the money due us while we can.

Chapter 5

We left the girls on the beach a short while ago. They wanted to grab another hour of sun before they headed up to shower, and we decided to get ours out of the way. It's almost one thirty, and we all agreed to skip lunch and go for a late afternoon dinner.

Vinny doesn't have a separate stall shower on his boat, and he prefers to use the old ones down by the main bathrooms instead of mine. Not because he doesn't appreciate the contrasting cleanliness or stronger water pressure, but even the remote chance of bumping into an attractive young woman is much more appealing to him than the privacy and comfort of my boat. He just walked by a minute ago with a big smile on his face, heading back to his boat to finish dressing and grab the seafood. From the look on his face, he has once again managed to meet someone of interest.

I'm already showered and relaxing a moment before the work begins. I've got on some khaki colored beach shorts that are fairly casual, and a soft blue Tommy Bahama shirt with a pattern of palm trees and a button down collar. It's a bit dressier than the shorts, but not too much.

I used one of the toilets in the marina's main bathroom myself when I first got back from the beach, and I ran into my buddy Dave again on the way out.

He had a few friends with him that must have come over on the ferry, and it appeared like they'd already been doing some drinking. They were all big boys, and I sense from the crap they were talking, more than a little cocky. I got the impression he was telling them something unpleasant about me, but I wasn't sure so I let it slide.

Right now I'm trying to forget about it and enjoy the beautiful afternoon. I poured myself a cold glass of chardonnay, and I'm sitting on one of my new deck chairs in a shaded area of the cockpit. A boat with a cockpit is sort of like having a porch when you're over here. It's a great place to sit and watch people, and it often leads to conversation with someone passing by. The laid back mood of most people here seems to encourage it.

There's a teenage volleyball game under way in the sand behind the Dock Master's shack, which is getting more competitive by the minute. Looking to my far right I see a group of youngsters swarming over the various playground toys and attractions. Adjacent to that is the small crowded bayside beach that the younger families tend to favor, a number of colorful beach chairs and umbrellas are dotting the sand. A few barbecue grills are still smoking with activity, but lunch is over for most. I hear a blender racing away from somewhere not too distant, and the call of a seagull has just finished off the lazy, hazy feeling of the afternoon nicely. Not that I care much for seagulls. As far as I'm concerned, they're nothing more than flying rats. But I somehow wouldn't find the experience of being on the water complete without the sound of those things crying out every now and then.

A loud voice breaks the relative serenity, and it's instantly recognizable. This guy is such a pain in the ass. His nickname is "Do-Be-Do", and he occupies most of his time by sticking his nose into everyone else's business.

Here he comes, arms waving in the air, barking out what sounds like docking instructions to a newly arriving boat. Instructions that I'm sure should be ignored if the person piloting the thing has any clue as to what they're doing. *Do-Be-Do* is actually the name of the man's boat, but it seems to fit him a lot better than his real name, which is Lenny. That happens sometimes.

At sixty some odd years old, and skinny as a rail, he's presently wearing his customary beach attire; a large beat up straw hat, and one of those tight brief Speedo bathing suits. His squirrelly little face is covered with several days of unshaven silver growth, and his grimace reveals a set of teeth that are small and randomly scattered across his upper and lower gums. From a distance, I would say *comical* is about the only way to describe the look. Up close, *scary* works better.

As self appointed mayor of the marina, he'll talk more nonsense than Carter has pills if you let him, and he can be intimidating to younger boaters that venture here for the first time. He rants and raves about one thing or another, and does it with the zeal of someone possessing real authority. The name of his boat might suggest to some that he's a huge Sinatra fan rather than a burned out pothead from the seventies. My guess is that he's not only the latter, but at some point he got a hold of some really bad stuff. His brain is at least half fried.

He's half jumping past my boat now all in a huff, heading towards the Dock Master's shack in his own little world. Flustered that someone has yet again chosen to ignore him. He'll get over it shortly though, and soon be off in a different direction, creating as much mayhem and havoc as any one man his size is capable of instigating.

Vinny and I docked right next to him for a whole weekend once, and by Sunday afternoon Vinny was ready to sink the guy's boat.

All becomes quiet once again as he goes, and I now see my old friend George Brenner stepping from a boat owned by one of his drinking buddies. I saw him walking that way from inside my cabin a few minutes ago, and I'm sure he was looking for ice. He's now stirring a glass pitcher full of half frozen clear liquid, and I know from experience we're talking about vodka martinis here. He pauses for a moment as he nears my boat, passing his large nose closely over the edge of the pitcher, that distinct smile of his occupying most of his face as he savors the familiar smell. He's big and jovial looking even when he's not smiling, with stark white hair that's combed straight back over his head without a part.

The Charms Of Fire Island

I've known George a long time, and he can be a pretty funny guy when he's not hammered. The problem is, he's always hammered. Retired for several years now, he was once a financial auditor for a large defense contractor that we still do business with, and he's been through my company books on more than one occasion. Very sharp with numbers, and in his heyday, a force to be reckoned with if you somehow managed to piss him off.

"How's that bouquet George?" I'm using the terminology I know he's fond of. I can't help but share his enthusiasm.

"Michael! This is one of my *best!*" he says with conviction, "grab some glasses my friend."

I hold up my wine glass. "I appreciate the offer George, but I'm doing wine this afternoon, and I'm about ready to start cooking an early dinner."

"Very well then," he's only marginally disappointed, "but never say I didn't offer."

"You know I'd never say such an awful thing about you George."

"Be good Michael." He's off again, probably to find some shade and the drinking partner he came close to abandoning.

"You too George."

I remember that guy being able to consume three or four gin martinis during a business lunch, and then go back to work like it was nothing. His favorite boast was that his boss didn't mind him drinking at lunch, as long as he didn't drink vodka. As he himself would mimic his boss: "George! The reason you're not allowed to drink vodka at lunch is because it doesn't smell enough on your breath. And when you go back to work in the afternoon it's important for people to know you're drunk. If they don't know you're drunk, they're going to think you're stupid; and no matter what George, I don't want anybody thinking I've got stupid people working for me."

He would roar with laughter every time he told that fabricated story, and regardless of the audience, it was always contagious.

The pleasant memory begins to fade, and I take a sip of wine as I feel my smile losing steam. Try as I might, I can't seem to get Dave Preston or Jill off my mind. I was up on the bridge of the boat earlier, draping my beach towel over one of the bench seats to dry, and I saw him and his buddies crowding the dock behind his boat - acting like they own the place, intentionally making it difficult for people to pass. That kind of thing annoys the hell out of me, and when I throw it in the mix with the earlier wisecrack he made about me, and then how he grabbed Jill forcefully enough to make her cry out in pain, it's about all I can take.

I've been good for so long, and I know I should stay right where I am, but I'm unable to resist the urge. Besides, Vinny might need some help carrying the seafood. Standing up, I finish what's left of the wine, and then give the muscles in my arms and legs a quick stretch, getting more committed to this new adventure by the second.

I make the turn at the corner of the dock, and I size up the group as I walk towards them. The four girls are sitting in the sand to the left of the dock, chatting away as women sometimes do. I see Jill making what appears to be a funny point as she pushes her right hand lightly against one of her friend's shoulders, and then she falls back into her lounge chair with both arms raised into the air as they all start laughing.

Her back is to me, and one of the other girls gives her a nudge as she sees me coming. I guess I must already be known to some extent among the women.

The guys are still taking up most of the dock, and as soon as Dave notices me approaching, he stands and turns slightly away, apparently whispering something to the others. I have a pretty good idea what he has in mind, and I couldn't have written the script any better myself.

"Ladies," I say nicely as I pass them first.

"Hi Michael," Jill responds. A look of concern is evident on her face.

"Beautiful day, isn't it?" I offer cheerfully.

"It sure is," one of the other girls responds.

I step over the first set of legs extended across my path, and straining to keep my demeanor as nonchalant as possible, I head pretty much straight for Dave.

He does exactly what I expect, and turns abruptly into me as I'm upon him. It's the old, "gee I'm sorry, I didn't know you were there" routine. The only problem for Dave is, the plan's about to backfire. I stiffen my shoulder and lean myself into the mass of his big body as he quickly rotates in my direction. A split second after contact, he finds himself sprawled painfully flat on his back, the beer can he was holding jarred free by the punishing blow. It's now rolling down the dock behind him, spilling whatever's left as it goes.

"Oh Dave, I'm so sorry!" I act like I'm completely surprised. "How clumsy of me!"

I extend my hand to him. "Here, let me help you up."

His three friends are out of their chairs in no time, one of them giving Dave the help he prefers, the other two starting to crowd me a little face to face.

"Hey, I think you did that on purpose," says the one to the left – he must be the brains of the outfit - a regular *genius*. He's a bit smaller than his friend to the right, but they're both every bit as big as Dave.

The one to the right now raises his left arm to point at me. "It looks to me like you fancy yourself a tough guy there hot shot," his voice is gruff, and a nasty grin forms across his face. "You want to get tough with me?"

He looks at his buddy with the smug look of a bully about to punish someone. I'm sure the only thing on his mind is figuring out how far he wants to go with it. At this point he's not expecting anything more out of me other than groveling.

I'm watching them both closely as I contemplate what I want to do. They are, in fact, some pretty big boys, and it's been a long time since I last rumbled. It's also been such a lovely day so far, and I know that whether I win or lose, I'm going to minimally suffer from muscle pain for at least several days.

The entire dock is now aware of our little conflict, and anybody that was sitting close by has already cleared the immediate area. Dave is almost back on his feet.

The big mouth right in front of me should go down without too much of a fuss; he's standing there with his legs far enough apart that a swift kick in the nuts should take him out. But then I've got to keep moving and swinging after that, because if one of them grabs me in a bear hug, I'm finished. I'm wearing soft sandals instead of my old shit kickers, and I don't think stomping on anyone's foot with these things is going to force a release.

I'm still in the process of contemplating all this weighty stuff, when suddenly my direction becomes clear. Using my most sincere tone of voice…

"I do appreciate your offer, but I think I'll pass this time."

He's looking at me like I'm pathetically hopeless, and not smart enough to realize he wasn't really giving me a choice. His arm starts to rise again with the index finger extended, and he's about to tell me something when I interrupt.

"But I'm pretty sure he would like to." I'm pointing directly behind him.

Before anyone has a chance to move, Vinny delivers a hard shot to his left kidney, and then grabs the wrist of his extended arm, twisting it back and hard to the right, forcing him to his knees before he ever knows what hit him. The guy screams out in pain as Vinny turns it some more, close to the point where the elbow joint is about to pop.

Vinny's manner is completely calm, hardly exerting an effort as he surveys the other three to see if they might want a piece of him.

No one does.

"Now I'll make all four of you one promise... If I ever see one of you raise a hand to this man again, I won't care if he chooses to ignore you or not... I will still personally break every *fucking bone* in your body.... Capeesh?"

It's not hard to tell they're all scared shitless, nodding their heads affirmatively. But then the *genius* starts to smile.

"Hey! What are we fighting about? You and me, we're *paisans!*"

He should have left well enough alone. Vinny releases the guy on his knees, and points at the genius, his finger coming up very close to the man's face.

"Let's get something straight asshole... I'm not your fucking paisan. And if you ever call me that again, I'll slap your ass silly just for saying it. Now you do yourself a favor, and don't open that stupid mouth of yours again until I'm well out of earshot. And even then, make sure I don't hear from someone else around here that you wound up saying something stupid behind my back."

He looks at the other three slowly, one at a time, a look of disgust on his face. Then he focuses back on the genius, the smile is long gone.

"You got that?"

The man begins to open his mouth, about to speak.

"No, no! Don't say a word! Just nod your head. I told you to keep the mouth shut. I couldn't stand to hear that annoying voice of yours again."

He nods so fast that it looks like his head is vibrating.

"Good... Good... Okay then." Vinny begins nodding his own head as he backs away slowly, unwinding himself from the moment as he glances around.

"You know Chenz - it touches me deeply that you worry so much about me, but I think I had the situation under control. I was just getting ready to make my move."

A smile breaks out on his face. "*You?* You think I was worried about *you?*" he's shaking his head to the contrary. "I know you too well for that Michael, and believe me, it was the *shirt* I was worried about. I just gave you that thing for your birthday a few weeks ago, and I would hate to have to tell you how much I spent on it."

Now, in a much lighter mood, he scans the crowd around us, "Hey! And what's with all the long faces? Okay... I apologize for my use of foul language in front of the women and children. It was not a nice thing to do. I was a little upset, and I'm sorry... Now, let's get some music going. Come on! Let's enjoy the afternoon!"

If nothing else, he is an entertainer. A couple of people start talking, I hear the first radio resume its previous volume, and shortly thereafter, it's as if the whole thing never happened.

I move close to Dave, so only he and the buddy next to him can hear me: "I don't know what your problem is Dave, but you should try to get over it. If for some reason you can't, come see me any time when he's not around," I nod in Vinny's direction, "maybe even try doing it like a real man, and come alone."

He says nothing.

I walk with Vinny over to his boat and we each grab one of the coolers from the cockpit. Then we head back towards the south dock, past the group once again. The men are all expressionless, and nothing is said by anyone as we pass.

The women look about the same as the men, and I'm suddenly feeling bad for them. Focusing quickly on Jill, I can see that her thoughts are somewhere distant, and she has no intention of looking my way. I feel like saying I'm sorry, but something tells me that it might be better for her sake if I keep my mouth shut. And besides, I'm not sorry. I didn't start it.

It's probably all for the best anyway. I'm sure that's the last I'll ever see of her, and that's the way it should be. I just hope I didn't create any further domestic problems for her.

Chapter 6

I hit the starters one at a time and the big diesels roar to life. I disconnected the water and electric hook-ups earlier, and removed all but two of the six dock lines. The wind is blowing slightly out of the south and against my stern, which keeps the boat safely away from the dock while I make my final preparations to leave. The only remaining ties to the slip are the stern lines, and once I throttle down, I nod to Vinny and Debbie to let me go. They each throw one into the cockpit.

"Thanks!" I shout above the noise of the engines.

Both of them wave goodbye with a look of sadness. I'm sure Debbie's is genuine, and I'm equally sure that Vinny just looks that way because he thinks he's supposed to. He gives me a wink as I make my final nod in his direction, as if I needed him to reassure me he's not really as heartbroken as he appears. Allison's somewhere down below in the cabin, evidently too distraught to even wave goodbye.

I shift both engines into forward, idling clear of the pilings, and then I'm heading straight for the mouth of the marina. Some lucky boater will be pleasantly surprised to find such a choice slip being abandoned this early on a Sunday morning. Rarely am I guilty of such a thing, but right now I'm in the mood to get home as soon as possible.

I notice Jill standing alone on the dock with her arms folded across her chest, watching me without expression as I pass in front of their boat. The Preston group walked by my boat last night without anyone even making eye contact, and I figured that's the way it has to be from now on. One of them was encouraging the rest of the group to walk a little faster or they'd miss the water taxi, and I heard another mention the name of a restaurant over in Fair Harbor. They were obviously headed there for dinner and that was the last I saw of them.

I can't help but nod my head in recognition of seeing her, and she unexpectedly lifts her hand free of her left elbow, waving it ever so slightly as she continues to watch me. I finally have to look away, forcing my thoughts back to where I was a minute ago, and recalling the reason why I'm leaving so early on such a lovely day.

We finished off a fantastic dinner late yesterday afternoon, not to mention a few drinks and almost three bottles of wine between us. Baked clams a la D'Angelo were followed by linguine with mussels in white sauce, and then we all tackled our own two and a half pound lobster. Well, we almost did. Vinny and I wound up having to help the girls finish theirs, but when it comes to doing chores like that, the both of us are always willing to sacrifice ourselves a little.

We all took a nice walk on the beach after dinner, and then it was back to the boat for coffee and dessert. Allison's mood had been noticeably more cheerful ever since she returned from the beach after midday, and I had assumed that whatever her problem was earlier in the day, she had finally gotten over it. After a glass of wine she seemed better than fine, and by the time we finished dinner, she was beginning to tease me, hinting she had some new lingerie in store for me later in the evening.

More than the physical aspect of it, I have always thought that great sex results from the pleasure shared by two people engaged in mental harmony, completely in tune with each other's needs, and getting at least equal enjoyment from doing something they know makes their lover happy.

I am personally a big fan of lingerie, and I think there is nothing more exciting than a woman accentuating her charms in such naughty and playful looking apparel. But it only works for me if the woman wearing it is into it as much as I am. That has never been the case with Allison, and I gave up hoping that she might change months ago. I have tried to put this incompatibility between us into some kind of perspective, discounting the importance of it overall, but at times I wondered if such differences were really all that trivial.

I bought her an outfit last Christmas to see if it might inspire her, but I've since only seen it on her once, and it was clearly a chore for her to wear it. I'm talking about a basic teddy here too, nothing close to the racy kind of stuff Gina used to wear.

The bottom line is, she doesn't like dressing up for sex, and it makes her noticeably uncomfortable when she does. That in turn has the effect of diminishing rather than heightening the experience for me, and so I just don't bring it up anymore.

With that being said, the fact that she went out on her own to buy lingerie was very exciting news. Considering her track record though, I should have realized something was up.

I feel my head moving slowly back and forth now with the sad memory of it all.

She appeared in the salon wearing this incredible looking dark-red fishnet cat-suit. It had a narrow vee-neck that extended down between her breasts, her nipples partially visible as they pushed against the soft stretched fabric on either side. Almost instantly, my attention shifted to the lacy trim that decorated the crotchless opening between her legs, barley held closed by a small bow of thin black ribbon. And then my eyes wandered slowly down those slender legs wrapped tightly in mesh, finding black high heels that were spiked and wild looking. Her smile was seductively inviting, and she began to tease me with an erotic motion of her tongue.

I was more excited than I had been in a long, long time, and I'm sure it was obvious she had my undivided attention. I found it impossible not to fast forward my mind to the moment I was going to open that little bow, and I had already told my fingers to forget about it. I fully intended to let my mouth have the honors of that heavenly thrill.

I was thinking I might have misjudged her. Maybe I was about to experience a whole new level of pleasure with her that I had never thought possible. Maybe she underwent some kind of profound attitude change, and this was only the beginning of a new frontier for us.

But then came the reality check, and I remember the exchange pretty much verbatim.

"You know Michael, if we were married, I'd be willing to wear outfits like this for you a lot more often."

The words hit me like a brick wall, and things pretty much went to hell in a hurry after that curve ball.

"*If we were married?* Is that why you're doing this?"

"Well…"

"Do you really think I'm that shallow?" I'm sure the disbelief and annoyance was clearly evident in my voice.

"Oh Michael, please don't ruin this moment. Don't you love me?"

"*Me* ruin the moment? No, no, no. I think you have things ass backwards here. Don't you think that a much more appropriate time to bring up marriage, or anything else for that matter, might have been *after the loving?*"

"No, I don't. Sometimes I think that's all you care about. And I'm not sure how much longer I'm willing to wait for some kind of commitment from you. I feel like I've been waiting forever for you to ask me to marry you. I thought that by now…"

"Whoa! Let's slow it way down here Allison… First of all, I've told you repeatedly since we met that marriage wasn't something I was looking for right now, and I resent the implication that I've been anything less than straightforward about that. Secondly, it's apparent you don't know me anywhere near as well as you think you do, because if you did, you would never pull this kind of crap on me."

"What kind is that?"

"Thinking you can use sex as a bargaining chip to get me to agree to something as serious as marriage."

"Well, it seems to be the only thing that gets your attention lately, and I'm not getting any younger."

"I'm sorry, I didn't realize that. But now that you mention it, I'm sure my behavior reveals something very important about the depth of our relationship, or maybe the lack thereof. Don't you think?"

She appeared surprised by such a direct challenge, and didn't seem sure of what to say.

"Good night, Allison."

I left her standing there, dressed like a million bucks, but no longer the least bit appealing to me.

With all of her things in my room, I figured she might be more comfortable there, and I decided to sleep in the guest cabin instead. I locked the door behind me, making sure she could hear me turn the latch, and nothing more was said until this morning.

I clear the No-Wake Zone in front of the marina, and I start to nudge the throttles. I have yet to open this baby up a little, and I figure this is as good a time as any. For some reason, I'm in the mood to burn some serious fuel. I'm tempted to jump it up quickly, but not knowing what she might be doing down below, I instead push the throttles up gradually and let the boat accelerate smoothly. The tachometers are soon reading twenty-two hundred RPMs, and the speedometer steadies at close to thirty-two knots. That's not too bad for thirty some odd thousand pounds of displacement. I'm glad I went for the bigger engines.

By the time Allison was up and around this morning, I was already making preparations to leave. I think she was anticipating some kind of reconciliation, and once she realized none was forthcoming, things got a little ugly. She started yelling, called me a bastard, said she couldn't believe she wasted a year of her life on me, and all sorts of other stuff.

She finished up by informing me that her mother had been right about me all along - whatever that's suppose to mean. A little extra shot that was meant to surprise and upset me I'm sure. I probably should have left it alone, but since she brought it up, I figured it was only fair for me to share some of my own thoughts in regard to her mother. I called her a nasty old bitch that was even more stuck up than her daughter, and I couldn't care less what she thought about me.

Unless I miss my guess, that exchange pretty much wrapped things up between us. As far as I'm concerned, that story is over, and I can't imagine she feels any differently.

I maintain my speed and make a wide turn as I approach Crazy Charlie. It's not quite nine o'clock and the bay is mostly calm with hardly a boat to be seen in any direction. I'm now heading almost dead north as I run alongside West Island. Once I pass the tiny island I'll be following the channel towards the northwest for a mile or so. Then I'll round the number eight buoy and head northeasterly, straight for the mouth of the Bay Shore Marina. This boat draws more than four feet of water, and I never wander too far from the main channels. If you run something like this aground, you're not only talking about repairs that can easily exceed twenty thousands dollars, you also lose the use of the boat for a while, and the season is already so painfully short as it is.

The remark Allison made about wasting a year of her life on me keeps coming to mind. Is that what I did as well? Do those of us in search of a soul mate really have any choice? I probably don't stop to think about it often enough, but I'm not getting any younger myself. I tell everyone I'm not looking for marriage because I don't think it's something one should focus on as a necessary destiny. In my view, marrying the wrong person is a lot worse than remaining single. But that doesn't mean I'm not hoping to eventually meet someone I truly fall in love with, and want to share the rest of my life. Maybe even have some children if it happens before I get too much older.

Realistically, though, what are the chances?

It takes so long to get to know someone, and then in a case like Allison and myself, it often becomes an ongoing relationship of convenience that lasts longer than it should. You know in your heart it will never go the distance, but you nevertheless struggle along because it's easier than the alternative, which is being alone most of the time, dating a bunch of different people that wear you out mentally and physically. You start becoming more anxious for sex, but at the same time you get more concerned if a new partner also seems too anxious. You don't know how free and easy they've been, and what kind of disease you could be getting yourself exposed to.

So as I reach the end of yet another failure in my attempt to find enduring happiness, I'm more convinced than ever that my chances of meeting someone who will satisfy me both sexually and intellectually like my ex did, are becoming pretty remote.

At least for the immediate future, I plan on enjoying my complete freedom for as long as it lasts. My good friend Vinny has never been married and I find it hard to believe he ever will. It doesn't seem to trouble him in the least. Being fairly rich and single isn't exactly the end of the world.

I shift my thoughts to the beauty of the bay, and I gaze off at the Captree Bridge, spanning most of the horizon to my left. Then as I close in on Bay Shore, a lone ferry rounds the buoy just outside the marina. She's on course for the east route around West Island, probably heading for Ocean Beach or Ocean Bay Park. It's a gorgeous morning, the boat is running flawlessly, and I take a moment to count my blessings before I start to throttle down.

I enter the marina at close to idle speed, passing the snack bar located at the very end of the long jetty forming the boat basin to my left. I throttle it all the way down as I make a left around the snack bar and pass the gas docks to the rear of it, and then turn right into Watchogue Creek, which is the canal I live on. I have yet to see any sign of Allison.

It's only a few hundred yards before the canal veers left and then right again, with my dock coming into view on the left side immediately after the first bend. I suppose it's a fairly small and modest home for someone of my present means, but it's on the water, close to the bay, and I've got all the creature comforts I desire. Best of all I own it outright. The entire property is no more than a quarter of an acre, and that's including the long narrow driveway that connects it to Bayview Avenue.

Watchogue Creek is also home to about half the ferries that operate out of Bay Shore, and one of the main passenger terminals faces my property from across the canal. In addition to that, there's a private boatyard and a gas dock just a few hundred yards north of me. It's not the most prestigious or expensive canal to live on in this area, but I personally love watching the boat traffic. I wouldn't be nearly as happy in one of those large mansions lining the quieter canals on the more expensive side of town.

The distance between the bulkhead and the house is no more than about twenty feet, and most of it's covered with ironwood decking. A cabana at the south end of the dock includes a well-stocked wet bar with a Tiki Hut facade, and there's an adjoining bathroom on the far side that works well for outside get-togethers. The dock has room enough for six large boats and a few smaller runabouts, but I stopped renting slips out years ago when I no longer needed the extra money. The amount of income is hardly worth the invasion of privacy. Vinny keeps his boat here, and so do a couple of other friends, but the rest of the slips usually remain unoccupied unless I'm having a party or someone stops by to visit.

I clear the pilings and back the stern of the boat slowly towards the bulkhead, suddenly wondering if Allison's okay. I thought for sure she would have at least grabbed one of the lines to give me a hand. Not that I necessarily need the help, but it's something she normally does to make the task a bit easier. Rather than wait, I descend the ladder and grab the two lines lying across the dock one at a time, attaching them to the cleats on either side of the stern. Then I secure the port spring-line before I climb back to the bridge and shut the engines.

As I turn to go back down again and check on her, she emerges from the cabin, stepping from the boat with her bag in hand, never bothering to face me.

"Call me if you feel like apologizing. Otherwise, I'll be back for my things when I get the chance." She continues walking along the dock with her back to me, heading for the small parking area along the side of the house.

That was pretty rude. "Please don't bother coming back," I call out, "I'll have everything packed and shipped to you by the middle of the week."

She turns to say something, but then I guess she decides against it. She turns away once again and disappears through the rose covered arbor leading out of the backyard. I hear her car starting, and then the sound of the engine racing as she guns it up the driveway.

I head for the bow and the rest of the dock lines.

Chapter 7

It wasn't close to the original plan of the day, but at least it was productive. After washing the boat down this morning I got in a good workout on the treadmill, and wound up having a late breakfast instead of an early lunch. I then spent a few hours at the shop catching up on some paperwork, followed by a trip to the car wash and some overdue food shopping.

I'm heading home now, cruising west along Main Street with the top down, enjoying the lovely weather. The downtown area seems to be looking better almost by the day, and it feels great to see the steady restoration that's taking place. Bay Shore was a center of economic and cultural activity back in the first half of the twentieth century, but unfortunately, the downtown area started falling into serious decay by the early nineteen-sixties. It's taken a lot of community effort over the past fifteen years or so to reestablish some of the original grandeur. Guys like me might donate some of the money, but I really take my hat off to the people who make that sort of thing happen down in the trenches.

I downshift as I pass Smith Avenue, making the left onto Bayview, turning up the stereo as soon as I leave the main drag. I enjoy loud music when I'm in the car, but I try not to offend anyone else with it, or appear too obnoxious.

Vinny called a little after noontime to tell me he was heading home around four o'clock, and wanted to know if he could join me for dinner. Something came up that Debbie has to do with her mother, so he's flying solo. If not for the fact that Vinny also told me the Carbone brothers wanted to stop by to show us something later, I would have suspected Debbie's story was a fabrication at his request, just an excuse to check up on me.

I had been kind of looking forward to a quiet steak dinner by myself, sitting in the shade of the deck, watching the boats go by, taking stock of my personal life and trying to figure out where I'm going with it. But I always enjoy Vinny's company, and I'm sure we'll manage at least a few laughs as we recount the "Year of Allison".

Frank and Joe Carbone are another story, and I try to minimize my exposure to those two as much as possible. I figured we'd be eating no later than five thirty, so I told Vinny to make sure they didn't show up before six.

They're a pair of tall, lanky, crazy ass twins, who couldn't possibly weigh in at more than a hundred and fifty pounds each, if they were soaking wet. Not that they aren't fairly tough for their size, but definitely more crazy than anything else. They always appear dirty and disheveled, normally wearing greasy work uniforms with their names printed over the left shirt pocket. Most people couldn't tell them apart if they didn't. Vinny finds them very amusing, but I honestly think they're a couple of certifiable lunatics.

We originally met them back in vocational school, and they now own a machine shop that does about four million a year in sales. While that's roughly a quarter of our size in volume, they proportionately employ considerably fewer people, maybe only a half a dozen or so unskilled laborers. Their basic operating philosophy is to control the business by doing everything themselves, and they possess very little in the way of managerial skills.

The last time I checked, their most important customer was Fat Tony, and in my opinion that's a pretty scary situation. But like I said, these guys aren't exactly rational, and I think they rather enjoy doing what they do, and how they get it done. It's simple for them. As much as anything else, they relish the reputation they have for being a little bit off their rockers, and they could never successfully mesh with the professional management of a larger, more sophisticated company anyway.

They both drive identical white panel vans as their main source of transportation, with the company name proudly displayed in large script letters along either side: *Carbone Brothers*.

Their idea of an employee Christmas party is a six-foot hero sandwich from the deli, a keg of beer, and a couple of hookers doing a strip tease for the boys in the shop. And when they throw one of their so-called dinner parties for their real close friends, you can't even believe what goes on there. Talk about live action, you want it, they got it; and they usually use a private room at a local restaurant, right under the nose of the other patrons. I made the mistake of attending only one of those sexual extravaganzas, and it scared the hell out of me. I kept thinking the cops were going to bust in at any second, and there I'd be on the cover of the morning newspaper, being led away in handcuffs. The caption reading something like, "Police Bust Suspected Head of Major Prostitution Ring."

Vinny thinks I'm too paranoid about these kinds of things, and I on the other hand think he tends to forget, we're not teenagers anymore.

A more recent episode of theirs took place at a restaurant up on the north shore of Long Island, which they had just started to frequent regularly. They were so impressed with the food, they convinced Fat Tony to make what he considers a laborious drive and join them there for dinner, thinking they might be able to score a few points by turning him on to a new hot spot. Unfortunately, the regular chef was ill that night and the food was awful. Tony of course got his jollies by busting their balls relentlessly about it during the entire course of the meal, and they finally got so embarrassed and pissed off that they couldn't take it any longer. After they finished dessert, the two of them got up and stormed the kitchen without warning, punching out the backup chef and one of his assistants that tried to intervene. I think they wound up paying them something like a grand apiece to avoid assault charges.

So I distance myself from them as much as I can, but ever since we first met them, they've had this thing for sucking up to Vinny. I think they value having a friendly connection with a guy as tough as he is, and I'm sure they at times do silly shit for no other reason than simply trying to impress him. Thankfully, Vinny doesn't encourage them too much, and that keeps visits like the one today at a minimum.

It has however been awhile since I've seen either one of them, and I suppose I'm a little curious as to why they're stopping by. But I'll find out soon enough, and I think I can handle the suspense in the meantime. I shift into second and push the garage door button as I hit the base of the driveway, punching the accelerator for one last cheap thrill along the narrow stretch of drive. I brake quickly as I approach the end, making a left into the right side of the open garage, bringing the Carrera to a stop alongside my Tahoe. I've had the Porsche for almost three years now, and it's been a lot of fun to drive, but the lease is up next month and this time I'm going for something with a little more comfort.

I enter the house from a rear door in the garage, passing through part of the dining room, and I drop my keys on the desk at the kitchen entrance. I see two messages on the machine and hit the play button.

The first one is my mom, thanking me for the gift certificate I sent her and my father for their anniversary. They're retired now in Florida, and I set them up at their favorite restaurant to celebrate the occasion with two other couples they've become friendly with. I always take them to this place when I'm down there for a visit, and I've gotten to know the owner fairly well, so all the certificate says is, "Dinner For Six - Soup to Nuts." He'll send me the bill later.

They have a problem with taking money from me, so I keep working at it in creative ways. On the one hand, it seems they have difficulty in grasping how well off I really am right now, but I think more than anything else, it's just hard for a parent to get recalibrated after so many years of perpetual giving and providing. I think its habit forming. Mom still sends me a check for fifty dollars on my birthday every year, and while I'm tempted each time to tell her to stop doing it, I instead always call to thank her and tell her how much the extra money came in handy. I'm sure she started to realize several years ago that I was exaggerating the reality of the gesture, but I know it nevertheless makes her feel good to hear me say it, and that's enough to make me feel good too. I love both of my parents, as much as anyone could, and I know how lucky I am that they're both still alive and healthy, not to mention self-sufficient. A number of people I know my age aren't so fortunate.

The next message is from Gary Wilson, my ticket agent, telling me he got the tickets I wanted for the Broadway matinee next week. Too bad I now have no one to go with. Maybe I'll give them to Vinny. He's due for an afternoon off during the week. I shake my head again at the thought of Allison and the rudeness of her final departure. I have to make sure I line up someone tomorrow to come pack her stuff and get it out of here. I don't want to leave too much of a window for her to come and get it in person.

With that thought fresh in my mind, I put away the groceries and then climb the stairs two at a time to my bedroom, figuring it's as good a time as any to get a jump on the collection process. Not that I think there's really all that much to gather up, but I don't want to forget anything. I'll give it a quick shot now, and then do it a few more times over the next day or so to minimize the chance of even the slightest oversight. I need to go through the boat as well, but not today.

It's almost three thirty when I finish making a salad for dinner. I grab a cold beer from the fridge and head for the deck with my newspaper. The rest of the meal will be simple enough - steak on the barbecue and baked potatoes. Vinny loves a good red wine as much as I do, and I think I'll open a bottle of the Phelps cabernet I picked up last week. I'm sure we'll tackle a bottle between us without much trouble, even if we do have work tomorrow.

There's a ferry just arriving back from the beach, packed full of people returning for another five days of either work or school. I'm sure most of them spent the entire weekend over there trying to unwind from last week, and now it's time to start the vicious cycle all over again. Many undoubtedly come from as far away as Manhattan too, so they still have a bit of a trip left before they reach home. One way or the other, you can bet they're all a lot less cheerful than they were on Friday.

I'm soon finished reading anything of interest, and before I bear down on the crossword puzzle I happen to look south along the canal towards the bay. At first it doesn't register, but then I see the name, *Second Time Around* on the transom, and I realize it's the Preston's boat idling away from me. It must have passed right in front of my house only a minute ago. Dave is on the bridge, but no sign of Jill.

I never saw them coming up the canal, but this is the only way out, so I guess they were up at the gas dock awhile. Gassing up a boat can take some time, and on a Sunday afternoon it can take forever just waiting your turn in line. That dock is a bit out of the way for many that use it, but it attracts some decent business by having the cheapest prices around. The quarters and dimes add up fast when you're pumping several hundred gallons of gas at a throw.

I watch until they're almost gone from sight around the second turn in the bend, and then I catch sight of Vinny, passing them on his way in, just as they finally disappear.

I'm trying like hell to stop thinking about those people, but they're not helping me out very much.

Chapter 8

"Everything is excellent as always. Thanks for inviting me."

Vinny and I are sitting across from one another at the table on the deck. The temperature's hanging somewhere in the low eighties, but the shade from the awning, combined with a slight breeze along the canal makes it feel quite pleasant.

"Just for the record, I didn't invite you. If I recall correctly, you invited yourself," I'm unable to suppress a grin as I say it.

"Oh yeah… I guess I did, didn't I." He returns the friendly jab with one of his charismatic smiles. "Well, thanks even more then. This steak is outstanding."

He grabs his glass and holds it up in my direction.

"To good health and great friendship."

I touch my glass to his and we both enjoy a sip of wine.

"This wine isn't too shabby either, I'm really enjoying it." He holds his glass up again to examine the rich red color. Then he slowly swirls it and samples the aroma before taking another sip. "I think I'm going to pick up a case of this stuff myself."

"You should."

He doesn't know it yet, but I looked at some preliminary financial figures earlier for our fiscal year that just ended, and our profit looks like it's going to be at least several hundred thousand dollars better than our last projection.

"From what I saw this morning, we finished up the year pretty strong."

"That's always good to hear. What drove the upside?"

"Higher productivity on the military work we shipped in the fourth quarter improved our profit margins by almost ten percent. The other big driver was the soaring price of titanium scrap metal, which of course we both knew about, but we were using it as a cushion against any negative surprises that might pop up. Fortunately, we don't have any."

"How much are we talking about?"

"Three hundred grand or more in total."

"That's a nice piece of extra change."

"Yes it is. But I want to review next year's budget again in detail, and make sure we haven't missed anything significant on the expense side before we enhance any of the employee bonus pools. I'd rather tell the accountants to put a reserve on the books now, instead of winding up with an unpleasant oversight during the year."

He shakes his head in agreement. "I understand. I'll go over my part of it again with the boys in the shop tomorrow, and we can review it line by line whenever you're ready."

"Good."

This is exactly why we get along so well in business. I know damn well that, just like me, Vinny would love nothing more than to maximize whatever current bonus he's able to get his hands on. There is nothing quite like good old fashioned "cash in hand". But he also never loses sight of the more important long-term objective, which is to manage the business for continued steady growth, and to the extent possible, making sure it's consistently profitable.

"Oh, and do me a favor... Make sure you keep Thursday afternoon open."

"Okay... What's up?"

"I want you to take a ride with me up to Mercedes."

He starts to smile again. "So you're finally going for it, huh?"

"Yeah, I think so."

"Man, that is one sweet automobile."

Vinny's a car enthusiast like I am, and I know he's been up to test drive the SL500 on more than one occasion. But I also know he's been wrestling with the sticker price for such indulgence. I felt the same way myself a few years back, before I decided it was time for the company to start leasing my cars. You see your net worth climbing nicely, and you know you can afford something better, but you keep asking yourself if it's worth that kind of money. He currently drives my old BMW 540, which I sold him when I first leased the Porsche, and it's still running like a champ. Better yet, it's paid for.

"*Sweet* is definitely the right word for that car... By the way, what color were *you* thinking about?"

I truly enjoy moments like this.

He looks honestly confused for a second.

"Me?"

"Yeah, you."

He looks at me evenly, making sure he hasn't in some way misunderstood me.

"No shit?"

"No shit. Well, as long as you don't insist on getting silver. That's what I'm going for."

Here comes that smile. "Hey Michael, I don't know what to say."

"So don't say anything. You've earned it."

He gets up and comes around the table to shake my hand, and then he wraps me in a bear hug.

"I hope you know how much I love you."

"I love you too, Chenz... Now let's get back to dinner before the ferry people start talking about us, or the Carbone's decide to show up."

We let go of each other, and then as he's backing away, he gives me a couple of affectionate taps on my left cheek with the open palm of his right hand.

"Screw all of them. I really appreciate this."

"I know you do... And believe me, it's my pleasure. Just keep taking care of business the way you have been."

He nods his head, starts to smile all over again, and then returns to his side of the table. "It's hard to believe sometimes how far we've come, isn't it?"

"Yeah, it is amazing, I think about it all the time. And the fact that we've done most of it together is truly the icing on the cake."

We continue eating in silence for a minute or two before anything more is said, and then I decide to shift gears a little.

"Hey, you think you'll ever wind up getting married?"

He's chewing on a piece of steak as he looks at me thoughtfully. He swallows it and takes a sip of wine. "Why would I want to do that?"

"I don't know. Maybe to have someone there for you all the time."

"Why would I want to have that?"

I should have known better than to start this exchange with him.

"So you're not running around all the time with somebody different, wondering who might be available to screw the next time you get horny. Going through the whole ordeal of getting to know someone, over and over again."

He smiles as he shakes his head. "Michael. Don't you get it? That's what it's all about! I can't imagine life without the variety. And besides, anyone I've ever known who got married, including yourself I might add, has never enjoyed the same intimacy after the fact."

He's got a point there. But I also know that with Gina, marriage had the effect of taking our relationship to a whole other level. I enjoyed being married to her a lot more than I did our life before that. Well, at least until things went south, anyway.

"What about when you become old and gray. What are you going to do then?"

"Providing I'm healthy? The same thing I'm doing now. In case you haven't noticed, there's an abundance of women, young and old, that are either single by choice, divorce, or because their husbands croaked on them. And if I'm not fortunate enough to stay healthy, I damn sure don't want some old bag doting all over me adding to my misery. You and I already have each other for that nonsense."

"You know what your problem is?" I ask rhetorically. "You've never been in love."

"Okay, maybe that's true. But where did it get you?"

"Ouch!"

"Hey, you asked for it."

"Yeah, I guess I did... But you know something... up until things unraveled, it was the most incredible feeling you could ever imagine. Spending time with someone that you love so much, you can't possibly think of living without them."

"Look, Michael, I understand what you're suggesting here, and theoretically speaking, I suppose that if someone were to ever come along and make me feel like that, I would want to marry them. But I have to tell you, I have a hard time believing that could ever happen."

"Well, to be honest, I'm also finding it harder and harder to believe it will ever happen to me again."

"So what's the problem? You're richer than most people could ever imagine, and you're a fairly good looking guy. I'm sure you could probably get almost any woman that you wanted into the sack without much trouble. Why not just go with the flow, and enjoy yourself?"

"I didn't know there was a *flow*."

"Oh, there's a flow all right, and it's going on all around you. All you have to do is decide if you want to be a part of it."

The sound of an engine in the driveway interrupts us, and we both quickly take a stab at our remaining steak. Then I hear two doors slamming simultaneously, and if there was any doubt at all about who might be here, that just settled it.

"Vinny!" a voice yells out. I can't tell which one it is.

"We're on the deck Joe!" Vinny calls back.

"No, Vinny! That was me, Frank!" he sounds a little hurt.

Vinny grins at me and shrugs his shoulders. "Well, it was a fifty-fifty shot."

"And I was just about to tell you how impressed I was that you could tell the difference."

The gate swings open and Frank's leading the way, with Joe only a half step behind him. What a surprise, they're both wearing dirty long-sleeve shop uniforms on a hot Sunday afternoon. Right now I'm able to easily tell them apart even without the help of their shirt labels, because Joe is smiling. Frank had a few of his teeth rearranged in a bar fight years ago, and all I have to do is line up the "Fs"- Frank, fight, funny looking teeth. What can I say, little things like that work for me.

Vinny gets up to shake hands first, and then he fakes a punch to Frank's stomach. "Hey! You know I was just messing with you Frank."

Frank smiles now too, and it's easy to see his teeth are status quo. "I knew that Vinny! It's good to see you buddy! Michael, how are you?"

"Not too bad Frank... Joe." I get up to shake both their hands. "You guys want a beer or something?" I'm not about to offer them any wine. The last time I remember them drinking an expensive red, they were chugging it down like it was water - I think trying to demonstrate to me, in their own misguided way, how much they were enjoying it. What a waste that was.

"No. Thanks anyway," Joe responds, "we're kind of on the run."

That's some of the best news I've heard all day.

"Yeah, but first we got something to show you guys!" Frank is beaming with pride. "Come and take a look at what we got in the van."

We follow them out to the driveway, and they both start scanning the area, checking to make sure the coast is clear before Frank reaches for the handle of the rear door. I suddenly find myself hoping to God this isn't some kind of a set up, like maybe they've got a couple of hookers in there, ready to pop out and entertain us right here in the driveway. But they wouldn't dare try something like that on my property unless Vinny was involved, and I'm sure he knows better than that. I look over at him just in case, but he looks as lost as I do.

They now swing both the doors open, and there's something in there that's large enough to take up most of the floor, bundled up in heavy moving blankets. Joe reaches in, and pulls a few of them out of the way.

"Recognize this?" he's obviously tickled pink, and he can't hold back a snorted chuckle.

It's a large bronze statue of a stallion, reared up on its hind legs, the front legs flailing forward, and the mouth wildly agape. It's got to be at least seven feet tall, and it appears to be very heavy. No doubt it's all solid metal.

Then it hits me.

"Is that the Global corporate mascot?"

Global Milling manufactures most of the equipment used within our industry throughout the world. They're a multibillion-dollar corporation headquartered in China, with a regional office for North American operations located just outside of Scranton, Pennsylvania. They had an open house this week that I chose not to attend, but I've been there a number of times over the years, and it's hard not to remember this striking statue adorning the main lobby.

"Yeah!" Frank says excitedly. "We took the fucking thing hostage!"

"You what?" Vinny's shaking his head, but I can tell he's impressed.

"Yeah," Joe starts to explain, "we picked it up after the open house yesterday. We were one of the last ones out, and there it was, just standing there all by itself with nobody around. So Frank backed up the van to the front door, and we carried it out."

He seems to sense that we could use some help in understanding why. "Hey, everyone knows about the new machine we bought last winter that turned out to be a lemon. We've been after them to fix it now for months, and all they keep doing is jerking us around. So now it's our turn to jerk them around a little."

"Does Lester Gordon know you got that?" Lester's the president of Global North America, and I know Lester well enough to know he's not the kind of guy you screw with like this.

"Oh yeah," Frank starts to laugh now, "he knows. We just got off the phone with him a couple of hours ago."

The Charms Of Fire Island   81

"Oh man," Joe adds, unable to contain his own laughter, "was he pissed! You guys should have been there... Frank starts the conversation by telling him that we have someone that wants to speak to him, and then he turns on this toy we picked up at the mall that starts whinnying like a horse."

"And then," Frank cuts in, laughing, "Joe tells him that if he ever wants to see the horse in one piece again, he better replace our machine with a brand new one by next week. And if we don't get proof it's in transit by this coming Friday, we're going to mill the horse's head off, and mail him the chips in a burlap bag."

Vinny starts laughing, and I'm not far behind him. I can just picture old Lester sitting in his big office getting an earful from these two, probably thinking at first that it's just a practical joke, or that maybe he's on Candid Camera. But, after he realizes they're serious...

I'm the first one to stop laughing. "Are you guys out of your minds?"

"What?" They both chime in at once.

"We paid good money for that machine, and it doesn't work right!" Frank exclaims. "What they're doing to us is bullshit!"

"Hey look, I think it's pretty funny," I tell them, "but based on what I'm sure this thing is worth, were talking about grand larceny here. And Lester Gordon didn't become the president of North American operations because he's used to taking crap from guys like you. He'll have them lock you up and throw away the key."

"Well, I'll bet you're wrong," Joe says. "First of all, Lester thinks we're crazy enough to do it, which we are, and he definitely doesn't want anything bad to happen to this horse. The big boss over in China sent it to him. Second of all, he's afraid of how much bad publicity he's going to get if he has us arrested, especially if the horse is nowhere to be found. Don't ever underestimate the power of an unhappy customer."

"All I know," Vinny jumps in, "is that if you two crazy bastards do decide to mill that fucking head off, I want to be there to see it personally. And I'm bringing my camera with me."

After hearing him say that, the both of them are beaming from ear to ear.

"You'll be the first one we call Vinny," Joe assures him excitedly, "and *that* you can count on buddy. I'm kind of hoping we get to do it too. But right now, we've got some more stops to make. We're sort of promoting our cause as much as possible, just in case the shit does hit the fan. And then we need to stash the horse someplace safe until we hear from Lester."

They slam the doors closed, give us a quick handshake goodbye, and then hop in the van.

I'm shaking my head as they make for the end of the driveway. And some people wonder why Long

Island has a reputation for having more than its fair share of maniacs in the machine shop business.

"Those guys are nuts," Vinny states the obvious... "But they are entertaining."

"Why do you encourage them?" I have to ask.

"I don't know. I guess because I can... But you know as well as I do that the two of them had a couple of screws loose way before we ever came along, so please don't try to hang any of the blame for that on me."

"Yeah... I suppose you're right about that."

Chapter 9

The ocean's as calm as the bay, with waves so tiny they hardly break at all, much less run up the beach. It's more of a slow, gentle lapping against the hard, flat sand of low tide. I can already feel the heat from the early morning sun against the back of my neck, and with summer barely underway, it's shaping up to be another scorcher more reminiscent of the dog days of July and August.

I'm walking at a good steady pace back from Ocean Beach to finish my workout, and it's coming up on eight o'clock as I near the empty beach and lifeguard chair at Atlantique. Knowing the serenity will be long gone in a couple of hours, I climb the few steps to the top of the landing and sit on one of the small benches, enjoying the panoramic view of sand and sea in peace and quiet.

It's Friday morning, and I once again decided to make it a long weekend. Only this time I'm doing it alone. Vinny claims he might make it over on Sunday, but it's doubtful. One of Debbie's cousins who live upstate is getting married tomorrow, and he's driving up with her tonight. By the time he gets back on Sunday, I'm sure a good part of the day will already be shot.

I'm sort of looking forward to the solitude, it should be a nice change of pace. I brought a few movies with me, and plenty of reading material. If I happen to get real lonely for some reason, there's always someone around the docks to chew the fat with, or maybe even round up a few guys and get a card game going. I also might take the ferry back home from Dunewood later, and bring my Whaler over to tool around with on the bay. It's a bit of a pain to jockey the thing back and forth, but it's always nice to have it over here.

Vinny and I had a good time at the Mercedes dealer yesterday, and it looks like we'll both be getting the cars we want in about two weeks. I knew all along that nothing as conservative as silver would work for him, and as I fully expected, he chose red with a cream colored interior. He was like a kid in a candy store, spending as much time flirting with our attractive saleswoman as he did admiring the car in the showroom. And five will get you ten, she wasn't being as friendly as she was just because we were buying cars. I'll bet the two of them wind up having dinner together well before our cars ever get here.

My mind has been wandering almost everywhere this morning, and I've been unable to focus on much of anything other then the phone call from Gina last evening. That was the first time she's called me since the divorce, so it's been almost five years now.

I was surprised to learn she had been keeping somewhat of a tab on my social life; evidently a friend of a friend knew Allison, and she had already heard about our breakup.

I wonder how such news manages to get around so fast.

She claimed her main reason for calling was just to make sure I was okay, but she also made it rather clear that she wanted very much to see me again, and hoped that at some point I might consider giving her another chance.

I always thought the day might come when she would call me herself, and I never expected it would faze me in the least, figuring that the bitter memories would far outweigh any fond ones. But it wasn't like that, and I was really surprised at how emotional it was for me to hear the sound of her voice again after such a long time. It was soft, sorrowful, submissive, and it fueled a tremendous rush of pleasant memories. Memories of so many wonderful times and intimate moments we shared. It's impossible to completely stop loving someone that once touched you so deeply.

I'm pretty sure she would have jumped at the chance to spend the night with me, and the thought of it did cross my mind: getting to know one another again between the sheets of my bed, mentally lost for hours in intense pleasure.

But I also knew that once I was sexually satisfied, the bad memories would take over before long, and I couldn't let myself go there. I miss making love to her so much it's scary, but I know at this point I could never trust her, and I couldn't even think of intentionally exposing myself to such pain again.

I am glad she called, though, instead of just showing up at my door, because I'm not so sure I could have been that strong in person.

Unfortunately, one thing is for certain; between Allison's unfinished tease last weekend, and then getting that phone call from Gina, to say I'm feeling a little bit of excess pressure in the lower half of my body would be one hell of an understatement. I've got to get my brain recalibrated as fast as I can, because I think I might be doing this *solo thing* for a while. I can't even think of anyone I'm interested in dating right now, much less being involved with sexually.

I get up and start walking towards the boat, tucking my newspapers under my left arm as I unscrew the cap of the water bottle to finish what's left. I toss the empty container in the first wastebasket I pass near the shuttered snack bar.

In spite of my trepidations, the thought of calling Gina back this morning flashes quickly through my mind, but then I dismiss it just as fast. I'm not only committed to a weekend of solitude, but I'm going to make sure my life keeps moving in a forward direction. There is absolutely nothing to be gained by chasing after something that has already failed me so miserably.

Chapter 10

The south dock of Atlantique's main basin has a ferry pier located pretty much in the center of it, sort of an extension to the walkway leading directly to the ocean. I'm docked on the east side of the pier this week, which draws a bit more foot traffic than the west. The boardwalk here feeds the entire second basin of the marina as well. Overall, the marina looks to be about half full, and I'm sure that by tomorrow, it will once again be at capacity, the same as last week.

After a long cool shower, I'm relaxing in the shade of the cockpit with my newspapers, wearing nothing more than a bathing suit. It's only around ten-thirty, but the temperature's already somewhere in the mid to upper eighties, and it's very humid.

I've seen a bunch of familiar faces walking by this morning, but there have also been many that I've never seen before. This place is becoming noticeably more popular by the year. Vinny called to check in a few minutes ago, and everything's running fine at the shop. More than anything else, he wanted to let me know that Lester Gordon caved in, and the Carbone's are getting their new machine in exchange for safe return of the horse. He was genuinely disappointed he wouldn't get to see them machine the head off that thing, and I have to admit, it would have been pretty funny to see. I still can't believe they got away with it. Old Lester must be getting soft on us.

I was off to a surprisingly good start on the more difficult crossword puzzle, but after the last couple of guesses I was forced to make, I can see that some of the resulting crosswords can't possibly be right, and I'm starting to fade fast.

"Any chance you're here by yourself?"

She catches me completely by surprise. I was so absorbed, I didn't see her coming down the dock. I don't even know from what direction she came. But there she is, looking as beautiful as ever, a beach chair in her right hand, and a canvas bag hanging over her left shoulder. Today's cover-up is plain white, and it barely falls far enough on her body to reach the bottom of her rear end. Her hair is up in a bun, with a dark blue plastic clip holding it in place.

What a smile.

At first it doesn't occur to me, but then as I continue to stare, I realize I'm not sure if I've answered her yet.

"Are you speaking today, Michael?" she asks me nicely.

I guess there's my answer. That was not good.

"Yes!" I say firmly, as I snap out of it and rise from my chair, "I'm sorry… my mind was elsewhere."

"Yes, you're talking? Or yes, you're here by yourself?" she teases me.

"Both... And I'm sure of it." I smile. "Why? What are you up to?"

"I came to see you."

"You did?" This woman has shocked me once again, and I'm not immediately sure what else to say.

"Where's Dave?"

"On his way upstate to a car show with his drinking buddies. I came over on the ferry." She nods towards the ferry pier.

I didn't even hear it arriving.

"He thinks I'm spending the day over at Robert Moses, and that's where I was headed. But I passed by your house and saw the boat was gone, so I took a chance you were here by yourself like last Friday."

"I see." I really don't, and I'm still a bit dumbfounded. I am, however, finding it quite intriguing that she's ventured this far out of her way just to see me.

"I hope you don't mind."

I must have been staring like a deer in headlights again.

"Uh… no, no, not at all. Here, please, let me help you." I hold out my left hand to take the chair first, and then offer my right to help her step aboard.

"Thank you," she says leaning towards me, giving me a peck on the cheek.

"You're welcome... Can I get you anything?"

She makes a cute face, scrunching her nose a little. "Is it too early for a glass of wine?" The tone of her voice sounded concerned with what I might think.

"Probably," I smile, "but I think that under the circumstances, I could use one myself."

I open the door to the cabin, and then turn to her. "Do you want to put your bag inside?"

"That would be nice. And if you don't mind, I'm taking off this cover-up."

"Please, make yourself comfortable."

While I have no reason for getting unnecessarily excited, I am finding myself anxious to see what's underneath it, fully aware that the last thing I need right now is another lustful temptation, but I can't seem to help myself. What in the world is she doing here?

I hold the door open and she leads the way inside, walking over to the couch to drop her bag. I pass her to the right and head for the small cooler in the galley where I have a couple of bottles of pinot grigio on ice. I open a bottle and fill two glasses about half way, then turn back towards the salon. She's waiting for me over by the couch, standing there with a smile. My eyes instantly wander over the very sexy bathing suit I haven't seen before. It's even more revealing than the others I've seen her in. Solid navy blue in color, with two tiny strings leading from the small triangle of fabric that's almost lost between her legs. They angle up from there and form little bows on each side of her waist. There's another bow tied between her sumptuous looking breasts, barely holding together the scanty material that only partially covers them. The last set of strings fall straight down from either side of her neck, appearing ever so slightly strained as they do their best to help keep everything in place.

I have to be careful here and try to shift my focus to something else, or there will soon be hard and undeniable evidence as to where my mind is. My god, she is beautiful.

"I bought this suit yesterday. Do you like it?" she asks as I hand her the glass of wine.

I could swear there was a teasing tone to her voice, but then again I'm not thinking too clearly right now. Either way, I better get her back outside as quickly as possible.

"To be perfectly honest, I think it looks incredible on you... Should we take our drinks outside?"

She smiles. "I was hoping you'd like it... Couldn't we stay inside for a while? It's much more comfortable in here with the air conditioning."

It feels to me like I have the heat on. She was *hoping* I would like it? What is that suppose to mean?

"Sure. I don't see why not."

I hold up my glass to hers. "Cheers."

"Cheers," she repeats, and we both take a sip.

"Santa Margherita?"

"That's very good. Most people I know couldn't tell the difference if they didn't see the label."

"I love a good bottle of wine, especially a good cabernet, when the right food calls for it."

"I'm impressed. Most women I know don't care much for red."

She smiles as she points her left index finger playfully in my direction, the same way she did it from the dock last Saturday morning. "It sounds to me like you don't know the right women."

"Touché," is all I say, and I offer her the end of the couch by extending my arm.

I take the single chair made of the same soft leather situated vertically to that, with the arms of the two pieces of furniture almost touching each other as they wrap the tiny corner table. Our legs are not too far apart, but I make sure mine are kept tucked in towards me. This woman is so easy to talk to, and from the way she handles herself, I'm betting she has a pretty sharp mind on top of everything else.

I'm not sure what's going on yet, but she definitely has my attention. And though it seems almost too obvious that she's in the process of making a pass at me, I'm sure I must be missing something. Even if it's true, I'm not sure what I should do. The fact that she's married doesn't sit right with me at all, but I'm suddenly feeling desperate for her ongoing friendly attention.

"How did you know where I lived?"

"I saw you on your deck last Sunday afternoon, when we were going by to gas up our boat."

"Oh, yeah. I noticed your boat on the way out, after you passed my house. But I didn't see you."

"I stayed down below on the return trip. I wasn't in the mood to listen to Dave talk nonsense about you and pretend like it didn't bother me."

"From the look on your face after my altercation with him on the dock, I had the impression you were never speaking to me again."

She reaches over and places her right hand on top of my wrist, squeezing it gently.

"You have no idea how good it felt to finally see somebody knock that son of a bitch on his ass. Believe me, I was jumping for joy on the inside, but I wasn't about to show it. I already knew I'd be spending another night on the beach by myself, and I didn't want to make matters any worse."

"No. Tell me you didn't. Don't you know how dangerous that can be? You never know who might be walking the beach late at night. Why didn't you just come visit me again?"

"As I recall, you had company, and I don't think she would have understood. By the way... Is what's her name heading over here sometime today?"

"It's Allison. And no, we're through with one another. That's why I left early last Sunday."

"Oh." She attempts to look sorry, but winds up smiling. "What a shame."

"Not really," I smile back. "We were together for the better part of a year, and it never did feel right to me... More wine?"

"Please."

I decide to bring the whole cooler over, rather than make another trip after this. It's going down too quickly for that.

"So tell me, can you fight like your friend does?"

"Like Vinny? No. Not even close. But I tend to hold my own when I have to."

"I thought I heard you call him Chenz?"

"I did. It's short for Vincenzo... But if you want him to like you, I'd suggest you go with Vinny. I think I'm the only one who's ever called him Chenz, and in my case, it's a term of endearment that goes back a long way. I'm sure he'd be hurt if I called him anything else."

"Well, you two certainly know how to make a scene. That's all I have to say."

"You should have seen us when we were younger." I smile at the thought, and take another drink. "We were always fighting someone over something."

She chuckles. "I've never seen Dave and his bully buddies so scared. But do yourself a favor, and watch your back, because he can be very dangerous when he puts his mind to it."

"Why, if I might ask, would you stay married to a guy like that?"

She appears as if she wasn't quite ready for the question, and I can see she's gathering her thoughts.

"In case you haven't noticed, he's an irrational, insanely jealous man."

"*Yes... That* I've noticed."

"Well, just between you and I, he once made me a very solemn promise." Her demeanor has become serious, and she's looking at me as if she's uncertain about continuing.

I nod my head, encouraging her to tell me whatever it is.

"He promised... that if I ever left him... he would hunt me down like a dog, and kill me with his bare hands... making sure that before I died, I'd suffer every bit as much pain as he did."

It wasn't hard to detect the fear in her voice. Wow! That's pretty sick.

"And you believe him?"

"Oh yeah. There's not a doubt in my mind he means every word of it."

I'm tempted to mention that there are laws designed to prevent such behavior, but I know how ridiculous it would sound. There are women like her being murdered every day by estranged lovers who went off the deep end and couldn't accept losing them. And that's with or without a court order of protection, which often proves meaningless in the cases where they're needed most.

"That's one heck of a catch twenty-two."

"Yes, it is."

She finishes the wine I just poured, and leans towards me as I reach again for the bottle. I'm starting to feel a little buzz, and I can tell she does as well. Her right hand comes to rest on top of my left, and I feel the tips of her fingers as they begin to lightly stroke me.

Maybe the situation with her husband should have me worrying more than I am, but I guess that bullies have always brought out the worst in me. I can't stand them. Plus I'm feeling very sorry for her, having to put up with such horrible intimidation, and the last thing I intend to do right now is pull away.

She takes another drink of wine, and then looks me straight in the eye.

"And to top it all off... the man is impotent." It was an emotional whisper.

I'm trying to make sense of what she just said.

"You gave me the impression he was all over you last Saturday morning."

"Oh, he was. Which makes things even worse, because he can never finish what he starts. And that only makes him nastier. Not that he was ever much of a lover to begin with."

She moves down from the couch and kneels before me, taking my wine glass and placing it on the table. Her hands touch me at the stomach first, sliding slowly up to my chest, and then they encircle the back of my neck. Her eyes begin to close, and her beautiful face draws near to me.

"Jill, I…"

"Michael, please…" she whispers desperately. "I can't remember the last time I made love to a real man. And ever since last weekend, it's impossible to get you out of my mind."

I can't believe this is happening. It's all starting to feel like a dream.

Her lips are soft but full of energy, and our tongues press urgently together as we hungrily taste each other for the first time. I'm simply unable to resist the temptation, and as we continue to kiss, my hands start sliding up along the sides of her body, eager to hold and feel the breasts I've yearned for. With her hands still clasped behind my neck, she leans away slightly to allow me the room I need, watching me intently as I enjoy the moment of initial touch. They're so nice and firm, yet tender to the gentle squeeze of my fingertips. I begin to rub her nipples through the thin fabric, and I feel the tempo of my breathing increasing, unable to contain my excitement. A grin of satisfaction appears on her lovely face, I'm sure the result of seeing how consumed I've now become with desire.

She reaches behind her neck to release the first two strings of her top, and I take care of the lower one. There's nothing but creamy smooth skin now surrounding the hardened nipples, and she sighs in delight as I gently play with them. She soon begins to slide slowly down against my body, kissing me along my chest and stomach as she goes, and just as she gets to the waist of my bathing suit, I push my body away from the chair and help her take it off.

There's a sparkle in her eyes as she kneels in front of me, her left hand touching me first and stroking me softly, her right hand massaging me gently between my legs. I'm going out of my mind as I look down at her, hoping upon hope she intends to please me from there. The thought of begging even comes to mind.

Just when I think I can't bear the suspense any longer, she smiles at me, and then begins to tease me by moving her tongue slowly across her upper lip. I feel the most incredible sensation as I watch her playfully lick me for the first time, and then as she takes me into the warm wetness of her mouth, I get this intense rush to my brain.

I'm mesmerized as I watch her beautiful face begin to slowly move up and down, her eyes engaging me every so often, her soft loving lips stretched firmly around me. This is well beyond anything I could have possibly imagined.

It's a nice steady rhythm at first, but before long she starts to mix it up, a few strokes of gentle sucking with light pressure from her lips and tongue, and then a flurry of firm intensity for several more. She now eases up once again, her gorgeous blue eyes peering steadily into mine, her lips then slowly working their way down and around almost my entire length. The sheer sight of it is amazing, and I'm stimulated beyond my wildest dreams as the warm snugness of her throat slowly engulfs me.

I feel it start to build from somewhere deep inside, and I'm certain we're dealing with virgin territory here. It's becoming so powerful that it's kind of scaring me.

Like an idiot I find myself scanning the area for a box of tissues. But looking back down at her, I'm pretty sure that tissues are the last thing she has on her mind.

"Oh my god!" I hear myself gasp.

I'm almost tempted to warn her about what I think might be coming, but there's no way in hell I could possibly break the mood right now, and something tells me that she has a pretty good idea anyway.

She shifts once again into high intensity, tickling me from down below at the same time with her fingernails, and I know I can't hold on much longer. It's almost unbearable at first, as if the release can't happen fast enough. My legs begin to shake uncontrollably as I feel the first hint of relief, and then the violent eruption begins, gushing from me forcefully, wave after wave, a seemingly endless torrent of pleasure. I hear myself grunting loudly, like an animal, completely lost in the moment. Nothing but pure ecstasy is racing through my mind, and the faint sound of her eagerly swallowing adds a dimension I couldn't possibly describe. Again and again the spasms rush through me, almost as if it will never end, and then I feel myself momentarily wavering on the brink of numbness.

I have no idea how long I'm frozen in that euphoric state of mind, but I do know that while I'm there, it's nothing less than heavenly bliss.

As things start gradually coming back into focus, I'm immediately certain of only one thing... I have never experienced anything even close to whatever it was she just did to me, mentally or physically.

Glancing down at her, I'm slowly regaining control of myself, but I'm unable to speak at first, my chest heaving rapidly as I attempt to catch my breath. Only now does she release me.

"I hope you enjoyed that as much as I did," she says sweetly, "you tasted wonderful."

"Oh!" I manage to only half gasp. "That was absolutely incredible!"

She smiles her contentment. "Good. I'm glad I could make you happy."

Happy? I think I'm delirious. I reach for her to come into my arms, and I hold her close for a couple of minutes, trying to calm myself down.

She's sitting across my lap with her head resting against my left shoulder, and my right hand is soon caressing her left breast. Then I begin to kiss her neck softly, anxious now to make love to her. Desperately wanting to satisfy her every bit as much as she just satisfied me, if that's even possible.

Sliding my hand between her thighs, I gently stroke her as I move my fingers slowly towards her bikini bottom. Her legs open responsively to my touch as I go. As I had hoped, she's soaking wet with excitement, and I can't wait to taste it. But I intend to take my time getting down to that pleasure, letting my mouth and tongue enjoy every inch of the journey.

She clings to me as I rise from the chair, her arms closely hugging my neck, her legs wrapped tightly around my waist. Our mouths press urgently together as our tongues wrestle once again, and then I turn to lower her into the chair, kneeling before her on the floor. I start at her neck, and kiss my way down until I'm lovingly licking and sucking on her breasts, her nipples are so hard and erect. I squeeze the right one gently between my teeth, and then soothe it with my tongue, glancing up at her as I do this several times. Her deep blue eyes are penetrating directly back into mine when the first moan of pleasure escapes from her lips, and then I feel the tender caress of her hands on either side of my head, directing my attention to her other waiting breast. I continue back and forth between them, one of my hands now taking the place of my mouth each time I do. She's soon breathing heavily.

Kissing my way slowly down across the flat of her stomach, I reach for the strings on each side of her waist, carefully pulling her bottoms down, and tossing them out of the way.

I move lower now, focusing on the insides of her thighs, licking and teasing my way to the most erotic place of all. I reach up to fondle her breasts, just as I begin a long stroke of my tongue, penetrating the thick creamy moisture for the first time. The taste is thrilling to me, and I'm unable to resist a sigh of pleasure as I look up at her, wanting her to know how much I'm enjoying myself.

She watches me intently as I do this, moaning deeply for more of the same, once again reaching out and caressing the sides of my head.

I'm careful not to dwell on one spot for too long, and continually change the motion of my tongue. One moment, the flat of it is slowly licking as much wetness from within her as I can, the next, I'm darting it quickly, barely inside of her, vibrating the tip of it as I tickle the very top of her opening. Then I press firmly into her, using my tongue and upper lip to nibble at her stiffness, playfully flicking it now and then to heighten the sensation.

Before long, she's moving in complete rhythm with me, pulling me ever more urgently against her. I bring her so close to the edge several times, but then back away as soon as I sense she might come too quickly.

"Please Michael! Please!" she pleads frantically.

I plunge deeply inside of her now, rubbing both of her nipples as I begin to lick her more passionately, and she's soon once again right on the edge. But instead of pulling away this time, I keep the movement of my tongue exactly where it needs to be to bring this intense tease to closure and take her completely over the top.

Her body trembles slightly at first, and then I can feel the pressure building rapidly. Her legs partially wrap my neck, and her hands grab my head firmly in anticipation.

"Oh yes!" she screams out. "That's it!"

Her body stiffens against my face with the initial rush, and each release brings a powerful shudder deep between her legs. Involuntary convulsions begin to consume her, and she seems to have lost all control of herself, her back bucking wildly against the soft leather of the chair. I reach around and grab both sides of her bottom, keeping her firmly pressed against my mouth, my tongue now completely still, doing nothing that would interfere with the natural flow of her pleasure. The feel and taste of her is unlike anything I can remember, and I savor every exhilarating second of the orgasm.

It finally subsides, and she falls back slowly into the chair, listlessly, appearing to be completely spent. I move up and lean forward to embrace her; she opens her arms to receive me, with the side of my head coming to rest against her chest.

We silently hold each other close, both of us drained well into a state of tranquility.

Chapter 11

I frequently marvel at how the culmination of untold thoughts in my mind at any given moment, can collectively result in such a prevailing overall mood. Right now I'm mentally wandering just about everywhere, both good and bad, but it's hard to deny that, all said and done, I'm totally content and at peace with myself. I can't remember the last time that anyone has so completely consumed me. In fact, I'm not sure anyone ever has. Not even Gina. I'll bet it's at least partially psychological - some kind of a fascination with the whole *forbidden fruit thing*. It was, after all, the first time I ever made love to a married woman. But even that element of the equation doesn't come close to explaining everything, and I see no reason to overly analyze such a great feeling anyway. Vinny's recent advice seems to fit the situation well, just go with the flow.

We're lying face to face under the sheets of my bed, her right hand tenderly caressing my left cheek. Our legs remain entangled, and our eyes are engaged in a rich stare of affection. A tear suddenly forms in the corner of her right eye, and I watch it as it runs down along the length of her nose, briefly forming into another droplet there before it falls to the pillow.

"Are you okay?" I whisper.

She nods her head slightly. "I've never felt so loved and satisfied in my entire life," she whispers back, "I just can't believe I have to leave you soon."

I wipe the tear gently from her face. "I was just thinking the same thing."

"Can I see you again sometime soon?" she sounds so fragile and unsure of her chances, innocently unaware of how deeply she's touched me.

"I certainly hope so. You've spoiled me so badly that I couldn't bear the thought of being without you for very long."

She smiles. "You're not so bad yourself."

It's nearing two-thirty in the afternoon, and we've been at it almost nonstop. We did take a breather at one point for a late breakfast, I rustled up some cheese omelets and toast; and we also managed to talk quite a bit between our bouts of passion. Not surprisingly, my initial impressions about her intelligence were very much on target, and meaningful conversation seems to flow so easily. We touched on everything from fine wine and food, to current events, sports and weather. But most of the time, we've been playing in bed.

I guess I should somehow be feeling guilty about the whole marriage thing, but under the circumstances I really don't. The only reason she's maintained that official status is because her husband has her scared to death, and as far as I'm concerned, that's immoral. I'm more convinced than ever that the only thing Dave Preston really needs is a major ass kicking, and the threat of additional punishment if he doesn't substantially adjust his attitude. Let him get a good feel for what it's like to be on the receiving end of some serious brutality. But I'm keeping my mouth shut right now, not about to say anything that could spoil an otherwise perfect day.

She told me earlier that he's in the used car business, and I plan on checking this guy out as soon as I get back to the office on Monday. The name of his company is the Preston Automotive Group, and it's located up in the town of Huntington, about twenty miles northwest of Bay Shore. They live over in Babylon, which is a couple of towns west of me, and keep their boat there in a community docking area. Once she mentioned the name of the business, I remembered seeing some of his obnoxious ads in the local newspaper. I think his slogan goes something like, "Let Honest Dave Help You Save", and he claims to be the most trustworthy guy you could ever buy a used car from. I'm sure it's all a crock of shit.

He's off with his buddies to an antique car show and swap meet in a small town upstate I've never heard of, supposedly making some very important business transactions. It sounds more like a boondoggle to me. He won't be back until late tomorrow night, but he's calling her at home around five o'clock, and he's threatened to head straight home to find her if she doesn't answer the phone. And he had the balls to call me a jackass.

"How about having dinner with me tonight?"

"Tonight?" she seems a bit surprised.

"Yeah, tonight," I smile. "Why? Do you have other plans?"

"No, it's not that," she smiles back. "I guess I just didn't expect you would want to see me again so soon."

"Well I do... desperately," I attempt a cute look of hopefulness. "That is if you want me to."

"Of course I want you to." She moves closer and kisses me.

"And I guess once I get that first phone call out of the way, I'll have at least a few hours of freedom before he calls again... although I think we better be careful. What do you have in mind?"

"There's a nice place off the beaten path in downtown Bay Shore, sort of an old fashioned bar and grill. Nothing overly fancy, but the atmosphere is friendly and the food is great."

"Oh yeah? What's the name of it?" she said it like someone who dines out regularly and fully expects to know the place.

"The Southside Hotel."

I can see she's drawing a blank, and I'm not surprised.

"Gee, I don't think I've ever heard of it. It's a hotel too?"

"No. It hasn't been a regular hotel for decades. But years ago, small hotels with a bar and dining room were very popular in villages like Bay Shore. Traveling salesmen used them as much as anyone to jump from town to town. Now I think they just keep the name to throw off people like you from outside the more immediate neighborhood. It's already too crowded as it is." I smile as I finish the friendly jab, and she responds by using her hand to playfully push at my face.

"Okay, wise guy. Then tell me this... if you take the ferry back with me, how will you get back to your boat tonight?"

"I could easily grab another ferry or bring my small boat back, but I'm not planning on taking the ferry with you. I don't think it would be a very smart move right now, and I have a better idea."

"Well, aren't *we* full of ideas all of a sudden?"

Her voice makes it sound like a condescending tease, but as she moves in close to kiss me again, I can sense she's happy.

"Do tell me," she whispers against the side of my face.

I don't know where any of this is headed, but I can't remember the last time I felt so good, and I'm not about to let the opportunity to see her again this weekend slip away from me. On the other hand, this marina is a real bad place for us to be getting to know each other. There are way too many familiar faces, and she is much too popular an attraction. Everyone here knows she's married.

I'm pretty sure that her quick entry this morning went mostly unnoticed. And even if someone did see her come aboard, they could only be guessing as to where she is now.

"How about instead of taking the ferry home, we try to minimize gossip around here, and I take you back across the bay on this. At this point no one could be certain that you're still on board. We'll have dinner tonight, both get a good night's sleep, and then we spend the whole day tomorrow anchored in the big cove next to the inlet. The water's calm and beautiful there, with plenty of room for privacy. I'll bring some nice food, we can swim a little if you want, or just relax in the sun. Maybe play some games, watch a movie, whatever. Get to know each other better."

I try to look even more hopeful than I did before.

She smiles. "You look so cute, like a little puppy dog."

"I'm trying my best," I can tell I amuse her. "So what do you think?"

"I think it all sounds wonderful... You don't know how much I struggled with the decision to come here today, and now I'm just so glad that I did."

"That makes two of us."

Chapter 12

I waved to a few familiar faces along the bar on my way in, but I didn't stop to say hello. Knowing this establishment as I do, I headed straight for the dining room, and it's a good thing I did. At about a quarter to six, it's already close to full, and I made it just in time to get one of the last tables for two. It's a nice small one off in the far corner.

Jill claims to be generally familiar with the downtown area, and once I explained the location more specifically, she felt she could find it without a problem. I also mentioned that I'd most likely be waiting for her in the dining room, in case she wanted to use the side entrance and avoid the bar area.

I got a bit of a scare when I first walked in, seeing a few of Gina's girlfriends at the end of the bar closest to the front door. Thank God she wasn't with them. I haven't seen her in here since the divorce, and the possibility of running into her never even occurred to me. I force myself to once again recall the glance I stole at the group as I entered, sort of as a double check, and I'm sure she wasn't with them. Her looks may not be as stunning as Jill's, but she is nevertheless a very pretty lady, and it would have been impossible for me not to notice her.

My Chivas on the rocks arrives, and after a sip of that, I pick up the menu with the daily specials and give it a once over. I'm feeling so damn good about Jill, and I can't wait to see her again. Once I had the boat well clear of Atlantique this afternoon, she came up on the bridge to join me for the ride back across the bay, staying close to my side and massaging me in one place or another the whole way home. She seems to know exactly how to touch me, and make me feel so incredibly special. If I hadn't experienced it first hand, I wouldn't have believed such a combination of beauty, intelligence, and sexuality even existed.

"Don't tell me you're having dinner all by yourself?"

Uh oh. That voice I know, and it doesn't belong to Jill. I look up slowly, trying my best to smile with enthusiasm.

"Gina! What a nice surprise!" I lie as I rise from my chair. "I hope I didn't somehow miss you on the way in."

"Nope," she smiles, "I just got here about two minutes ago."

She's all bubbly, and appears quite happy to see me. A few inches shorter than Jill, she has a great figure as well, but keeps her blonde hair short and blown back, similar in style to the way Allison does it. Her green eyes are sparkling just the way I remember them, and I have to admit that the expression she's wearing along with the smile is adorable. I'm surprised to see the small diamond necklace I gave her before we were married. It's hanging into the open vee neck of a pink polo shirt, and she's wearing that with a pair of washed out jeans that wrap tightly around her slender waist.

"Roseanne said she saw you come in by yourself, and I thought I'd come say hello. Any chance you're looking for company?"

"Uh, no... Sorry. I'm meeting someone."

"Oh." Her look saddens.

And wouldn't you know it, Jill just walked in the side door and she's coming right at us. She's dressed to kill too. A skimpy light blue summer dress that falls about halfway down her long lovely legs, a small bow gathering the sheer cotton top of it just barely enough to cover her breasts. Most of her hair is up in a bun, but a few stray wisps curl down along the sides of her beautiful face.

A number of eyes follow her as she crosses the room, I see the guy sitting next to the door getting a sharp slap from his female companion. It wasn't playful.

Gina's back is turned slightly towards her, and she doesn't see her coming at first. She's saying something about how good it is to see me, but my focus has clearly shifted and I don't catch it all. I try to help her avoid complete shock by softly clearing my throat, and I nod my head in Jill's direction. This is getting worse by the second.

"Hi Jill!" I do my best to sound lighthearted, as if I'm casually running into one of my buddies, but as soon as Gina catches sight of her, the shock on her face is evident.

"Jill, this is Gina. Gina, Jill."

They instantly size each other up, and I think if looks could kill, they'd both already be dead.

Doing a lousy job of trying to look unfazed, Gina turns to me, "It was good to see you again Michael, I hope you enjoy your dinner."

"Thanks. You too."

I notice she doesn't wish Jill the same, and instead makes her way quietly to the door leading back to the bar.

I find myself honestly feeling sorry for her, but I'm not sure why. And why in the world do I feel guilty about her seeing me with somebody else? This is ridiculous. I hold Jill's chair for her, and then I take my own. My back is against the wall, which is where I like it whenever I have the option.

"Who was that?" her voice is pleasant, but I can tell she's forcing it.

"My ex."

"Oh... I see. She seemed rather upset. Is there still something between you two I need to be worried about?"

Direct, I must say. But she looks and sounds sincere. And if the roles were reversed, I would think it a fair question to pose myself. The fact she already cares enough about me to even ask, makes me start to feel better again. She looks so incredibly inviting, and it's hard to believe how deeply she pleased me earlier.

"No, not at all. This is the first time I've even run into her in well over a year. Believe me, whatever we once had between us was over long ago."

"Well that's good to hear." She reaches across the table for my hand. "After the way you made me feel today, I couldn't bear the thought of possibly losing you so quickly."

"The way I made *you* feel? I can't believe what a lover you are."

She smiles what has to be a knowing smile, "Good. I'll try to make sure you keep feeling that way."

What else could a guy possibly ask for? I'm suddenly thinking about what a terrific time we're going to have tomorrow, just the two of us, all alone for the entire day.

"Me too," I say, as I squeeze her hand lightly.

I order her a glass of the house cabernet, and she begins to survey the menu. Looking around the room, I see the kitchen door swing open, and out comes my old friend Ned Baker.

As a younger man he bartended here for many years, and after living up in New England for a while, he wound up coming back and buying the place. A number of years my senior, he's a very savvy and accomplished businessman, not to mention a good cook. He's also one hell of an entertainer, and a lot of fun to have a couple of drinks with. Almost always wearing a smile, he's a rather big and stocky guy who's lost a fair amount of his light brown hair, his full beard always trimmed on the shorter side.

He gives me a half wave as he scans the room, and begins to work his way over, stopping briefly to say hello to other friends as he comes.

I raise my left hand slightly in acknowledgment, and nod my head to complete the hello.

"There's someone I want you to meet."

"Just please don't let it be another one of your exes," she grins cutely.

I love her sense of humor.

"That's pretty funny. But no, I've only been married once... It's the owner."

"That's a relief."

He's coming at us almost from the side now, completely focused on Jill as he closes in. He finally graces me with a quick nod as he nears, registering an unmistakable vote of approval. The look at me is short lived though, and he turns his attention back to Jill. He's waiting for an introduction, but I think I'll delay it some, just to bust his balls for ignoring me so much. Not that I can blame him.

"Mr. Baker! How are you sir? You look thirsty."

I usually buy him a drink on the way in, and he gets me on the way out.

"Parched." He smiles briefly at the running joke as he strains his head in my direction, but I know he could care less about the beer right now.

I stick my arm out, in between him and Jill to wave over Kathy, our waitress, who I can see has overheard us and is already approaching with a grin of amusement. She knows very well why she's being summoned.

"Please get Mr. Baker here a bottle of Beck's before the poor man dehydrates. I hate when I see that happen."

She's no sooner gone when Ned decides he's waited long enough for me.

"I don't believe I've had the pleasure," he says directly to Jill.

"Oh, gee, I'm sorry Ned," I try to sound sincere. "Let me introduce you to a friend of mine; this is Jill Preston."

"Well, it's very nice to meet you Jill."

I'm sure she's already permanently etched into that memory bank of his. He has this uncanny knack for remembering names and faces, even the average ones.

"Thank you Ned. Same to you."

After all these years, I can tell just by looking at his expression that he's preparing to deliver some kind of a wisecrack; and sure enough, here he goes...

"It's certainly nice to see Michael with someone so lovely for a change."

"Why thank you Ned... how nice of you to say that."

He's such a charmer. No less at my expense.

"Watch out," I caution, "his next move will be to check your I.D... He gets to flatter you and find out where you live all in one shot."

I can't help but laugh a little at my own humor, and he turns to me with that signature smile of his.

"Be careful there Michael, or I'll have to share a few stories of my own. And I think I always come out on top when that happens."

He's right about that. I chuckle again at the thought of him when he gets on a roll, holding up my right hand to acknowledge the point, and agree that I'm happy to leave well enough alone.

He now takes on a more serious look, "You know I'm always happy to see you, but I'm surprised you're here on such a gorgeous Friday night. I hope you're not having trouble with the boat already."

"No. Thanks, it's running great. I've been at the beach all day and I'm heading back tomorrow. I just had some business to take care of this afternoon, and thought is was a good opportunity to have dinner here with Jill."

"Well that's good. I'm glad you came."

The beer arrives, and he holds it up for a toast.

"To you Michael... And Jill, I hope to see you here again soon."

"I'm sure you will," she replies before we all take a drink.

He nods in approval of the ice-cold beer, as well as to signal that it's time for him to get back to work. He turns to take his leave.

"Oh, and just in case you're heading for the bar," I interrupt him, "I've already had the pleasure of running into Gina."

He stops and turns back to us, holding his beer in the air, a grin on his face as he looks directly at Jill, "You see, that's why I love this guy. He's always doing his best to make my job a little easier."

I raise my glass to him, also grinning as we exchange a look of understanding. We both take another sip before he resumes his retreat.

"I like this place," she says with an air of certainty. "I feel right at home here."

"That's good. You hungry?"

"Totally famished. What do you recommend?"

"Honestly, everything here is good, from the burgers to the porterhouse steak. I had the veal franchese special they're serving tonight a couple of weeks ago and it was excellent. The seafood specials are always fresh, and the pot roast is probably the most tender you'll ever taste."

"I must say that's quite an endorsement, and it all sounds delicious. But I think you just sold me on the veal."

"Good. I think I'll have it again myself."

Chapter 13

I'm feeling something like the way I do towards the end of a great vacation; when the daily grind of regular life starts approaching rapidly, and I'm about to begin the long wait leading up to the next one. Only this is worse, because in this situation I have no control over when I might get the chance to repeat the experience. The last two days have felt like a dream come true, but I know that the aftermath will be equally depressing. It's coming up on three in the afternoon, and we have to start heading home soon. I have no idea when I'll see her again.

We're sitting on the bridge of the boat, side by side on the lounge seat, forward of the helm. My bare feet are resting up on the wind deflector and my back is comfortably angled into the seatback cushion. Her head's resting against the bare skin of my chest as my left arm wraps her gently into me. I feel her hand massaging the top of my leg beneath the fabric of my bathing suit, but I'm looking off into the distance, focused more on the striking blue water of the ocean as I reflect on things. It sparkles just beyond the thin strip of sandy beach that forms the east side of the Fire Island Inlet.

A mild breeze is blowing out of the southwest, and there's enough tension on the anchor line to keep us pointed steadily in that direction, pretty much straight at the mouth of the inlet. The sun is still strong, but the hard top of the bridge is shading most of our bodies. Smaller boats are scattered about, some fishing, and some resting on the hook like we are. A fishing charter is cruising in from somewhere in the ocean, apparently done for the day. Seagulls hover behind it waiting for scraps as the catch is cleaned, and well-adorned weekend anglers, now reduced to mere sightseers, are lining the railing as the excursion nears its end.

We had a fabulous time at dinner last night, followed by a brief stop by my place so Jill could see the house. The flow of conversation was nonstop and effortless, never forced, unlike anything I can remember since I first started dating Gina. We definitely seem to have a lot in common.

This morning she left her car in the community docking area at the end of my block, and I picked her up there on my way out of the canal. That's also where I'll drop her off later. I didn't think it would be very smart to leave her car on my property, hidden in the garage or otherwise. You never know who might happen by and stumble upon it.

We set the anchor here around nine o'clock and we haven't budged since. It wasn't even fifteen minutes later when we found ourselves in bed for the first time, and it was only about an hour ago that we untangled from the grand finale. I didn't think it was possible for a bathing suit to have any less fabric than the one she was wearing yesterday, but I was wrong.

This one's a tiny little thing in solid white, that hides almost nothing - and if it's mission in life was to keep me totally captivated throughout the day, it has done one heck of a job. I haven't been able to take my eyes off of her. And what a fantastic time we've had in between the throes of incredible sex.

Breakfast consisted of nothing more than coffee, and we drank almost a pot between us on the way over. She drinks it black like I do, which makes her the first woman I know to do so, and for some reason I find that pretty special.

Lunch was an entirely different story, and it was a regular feast. I had some jumbo shrimp in the freezer that I took out last night to thaw, along with a nice piece of chateaubriand. I grilled them both on the portable barbecue in the cockpit, basting the shrimp lightly with lemon and butter. I baked a couple of potatoes in the galley oven, and rounded it all out with a tossed salad and a loaf of Italian bread I got at the supermarket early this morning. We drank the last of the pinot grigio from yesterday as we prepared everything, and I brought a good bottle of red to go with the meal. It was the same stuff Vinny and I drank last Sunday. I could tell she was more than a little impressed with it. Probably not the kind of wine she gets to taste very often.

I can't even count how many times we must have laughed at one thing or another, and it wasn't only me telling the jokes or being amusing. She's always right there with me, and it's so much fun to be around her. Not only did she beat me two out of three times at

Yahtzee, she also helped me fix and finish the crossword puzzle from yesterday morning I had messed up so horribly.

I'm fairly certain that this is what you call true love at first sight, and just the thought of it makes me squeeze her a little as I glance down. She looks up solemnly to meet my gaze, almost as if she's reading my mind. Her eyes appears distant, but I can see she's about to say something. Her mouth opens as if ready to speak, but then it closes without a sound.

She starts again slowly... "I loved my first husband very deeply..." it's almost a whisper. "But even he was never able to make me feel the way that you have these last couple of days... No one ever has."

It feels great to hear her say that, but the "first husband" thing is a bit of a surprise.

"First husband? What happened to him?"

I can see her swallow hard, and moisture begins to fill her eyes.

"Officially?" her soft voice fails a little.

"Kevin was killed in a hunting accident. It happened a few years ago."

"Jeez, I'm sorry. But what do you mean by *officially?*"

She looks down and away from me.

"That's what the police investigation concluded."

"Okay... and?" I place my right hand against her cheek as she reengages my eyes.

"Guess who was with him when it happened?"

It takes a couple of seconds for it to register.

"You're kidding?"

"Please don't ever tell anyone I said that, because there's no way I could ever prove it. It didn't even occur to me at the time as being a possibility. It was only after the fact, when we were married, that I started to figure things out."

She pauses for a moment to gather her thoughts, owning every bit of my attention.

"Dave had been a close friend of Kevin's for years, and so it was natural for him to be around us a lot once we became a couple. He was always flirting with me in a playful sort of way, and occasionally even touching me in ways that he shouldn't have. But it was never anything too outlandish, and Kevin never seemed to mind, so I figured it was okay. Over time, though, it did become somewhat evident that his desires for me were more serious than innocent friendship, and I should have suspected him a lot sooner than I did."

"How did the accident happen?" I'm keeping my demeanor as calm as possible, but suddenly wondering how sick and dangerous this guy really is.

"Well, as the story goes, it was a freak thing - a stray rifle shot from another hunting party that was never found or identified. The bullet didn't come close to matching up with the only rifle Dave said he took with him, and so at the time it was hard to believe anything else."

"And then?"

"Dave doted over me like you couldn't believe when it first happened. He wouldn't let anyone else even get close to me, and he waited on me hand and foot. My family came in from Wichita for the funeral, but after they left, I felt like I had nobody to turn to but Dave. I was so distraught, and I guess he gave me the sense of security I desperately needed. In my mind, he had also lost his best friend, and it seemed natural for us to console one another. Before long we became intimate, and not quite a year later we were married. But almost overnight, the way he treated me changed dramatically. It became apparent rather quickly that he was totally obsessed with me, and he wanted to own and control me like I was a piece of property. That was over two years ago, and it's been a nightmare ever since."

"That's pretty sad. But such behavior in itself doesn't mean he had anything to do with killing your husband."

"No... It doesn't. But I accused him of doing it once, when we were having one of our nastier fights, and you know what he said?"

I shake my head without speaking.

"Almost nothing. He just stared me down with this sick looking smile for what must have been the better part of a minute, and then his only words were – *'try to prove it'*."

"Wow," I barely mutter it.

"Believe me, the look in his eyes alone was enough to convince me he was guilty, but I will never forget that evil smile, and the way he so arrogantly challenged me - I remember lying next to him in bed later that night, after he had fallen asleep, overwhelmed with hatred. I was tempted to grab something and smash it over his head, and kill him right then and there. But without any proof of what he had done, where would that have gotten me?"

I feel a chill run through me, "That's terrible."

"Yes it is. And it's the kind of thing that if you ever heard about it happening to somebody else, you'd say there is no way in hell you would ever put up with it. Just for starters, you'd walk right out on the son of a bitch and get a divorce. But let me tell you something - it's all very different when you're the one living in constant fear of what a vicious animal like him might do to get his revenge."

It sounds like I've significantly underestimated this guy, and I better figure things out very carefully before I engage him again. He's far from being the typical neighborhood bully I had figured him for, and a cold calculating killer is a whole different ball game. At the moment, though, all I can do is feel enormous sympathy for this intensely loving and beautiful woman, unable to fathom the horrible abuse she's been forced to endure. What I would give to have someone like her to share my life with - her wanting and needing only me to make her feel whole and complete, not the least bit interested in any other man. I'd do whatever it took to keep her happy.

"Don't worry. Somehow we'll figure something out."

She starts to sob as she presses more firmly into me, and I soon feel the moisture of her tears against my chest.

"I think I'm falling in love with you Michael... But I'm afraid. I don't want to live in constant fear of him killing me. I'm not sure what to do anymore."

I have to really nail this bastard. Maybe beat him half to death to force a confession out of him and get his pitiful ass thrown in jail for at least a few decades.

"It'll be alright," I try once again. "But you have to keep your cool for now, and maintain the status quo until we come up with some kind of a plan... Okay?"

She lifts her head and looks directly into my eyes, nodding her agreement as she bites slightly on her upper lip, traces of tears line both of her cheeks.

"Okay."

Her words continue to echo softly in my mind: *I think I'm falling in love with you Michael*.

Chapter 14

A nerve is struck hard somewhere deep inside of me, and my body jumps violently from the mattress, shocking me into consciousness.

"Ugh!" I blurt uncontrollably as it happens, mentally jarred by the enormous trauma.

I feel the sweat running down from both sides of my face before I even touch it, and then the pillow beneath me, which is saturated. That felt so real it was scary.

My breathing is heavy but quick, and I lie there for a while unable to move. More than anything, feeling relieved it was only a dream.

I was in a strange forest, running from Dave as he hunted me down. I was wearing a bright orange hat and vest, both of which had a black bull's-eye pasted on the front and back. The weirdest part was that I put them on because Dave asked me to. He said it would be a lot more fun for him to hunt me if I did. I was running as fast as I could, and at first I wasn't going anywhere, like a cartoon scene when you keep seeing the same background over and over again. I was a sitting duck, right out in the open. A few shots had already come close to taking my head off, and I was sure that any second it was over for me. But then I started seeing the scenery change, and I knew I was moving again. The trees started getting bigger and they were becoming more dense. I was beginning to think I was free and clear when I suddenly ran into a brick wall, literally. I was at the end of an alley somewhere in the city, surrounded by tall red brick buildings with nowhere to go. No doors to try, no fire escape ladders to jump for. Trapped like a rat. Turning back to see if he'd been able to follow me, there he stood only twenty feet away. He had me dead in his sights, aiming directly at my head. I could see a slight smile on his face, and the movement of his finger as he slowly squeezed the trigger.

Oh my god, that was awful.

I sit up for a moment and shudder slightly, letting the unpleasant memory drain from within me. A look at the alarm clock tells me it's three in the morning, and after only a second or two I remember which one. Sunday.

It was less than twelve hours ago when I watched her drive slowly away from the dock, waving goodbye as she wiped tears from her eyes.

How is it possible that I feel so lost without her company? Worried about where she is right now, whether she's safe or not. It was only three days ago that she wasn't even a part of my life.

Chapter 15

"*Hey!* You were the one who told me I should loosen up and go with the flow. And now that I'm finally going, all you can do is give me shit about it?"

"I'm not giving you shit Michael, I'm only making the point that you could have made a less complicated choice. There's a reason I didn't include married woman among my list of abundantly available females, and that's because they're not. They're married."

"Now hold on. I didn't choose her, she chose me. And she freaking seduced me right there on my boat! There was no way I could possibly refuse her."

I know I sound like a kid after getting laid for the first time, but I can't help myself.

"Chenz, I'm telling you, this woman is unlike anything I could have ever imagined. Not only is she unbelievable in bed, she's got this awesome personality. And to top it all off, there's a pretty sharp mind inside of that incredible body."

A smile comes to my face as I finish the sentence, unable to suppress how good the thought of her makes me feel.

We're over at a bayside bar in Kismet, the first town east of the lighthouse. Vinny got back from the wedding a few hours ago, and we took a ride here on the Whaler so I could fill him in on the events of the weekend. Sitting across from one another at an outside table near the docks, we have a nice view of the boats coming and going from the boat basin just a few steps away. A big green Heineken umbrella shades us from the afternoon sun.

He studies me for a moment, taking a sip of beer, and then begins to nod his understanding and acceptance of the situation.

"Well I have to admit one thing. I haven't seen you even close to being this excited about a woman since you first started dating your ex, and it sounds to me like she has every reason to be cheating on that dirt-bag she's married to."

I'm very glad to hear him say that.

"So you're with me on this?"

"What kind of a question is that? Of course I'm with you. I just want you to remember how much we both have to lose if you do something foolish to this guy and wind up going to jail over it. Or worse yet, you get sloppy and he winds up doing something nasty to you."

"I know Chenz... I know." It's all I can seem to think about since that nightmare shocked me into consciousness this morning. "There's got to be a way to neutralize him without getting burned over it."

"I'm sure there is. But we have to take it slow and make sure we know exactly what we're dealing with before we go off on a tangent."

"I couldn't agree more... What do you suggest for starters?"

He looks thoughtful for a moment.

"Why don't you call Peter Long and have him do a thorough background check on Mr. Preston. Find out whatever you can about his business and financial situation."

Peter Long's a private investigator we've used on occasion. He's doesn't come cheap, but he's very good.

"Yeah, I was thinking the same thing myself."

Vinny starts to smile, "And *maybe*... I'll send the Carbone brothers out shopping for a used car. Have them snoop around the place and see what they can find, take Dave for test drive or two, and just generally screw around with him a little to see what kind of reaction they get. You never know what they might turn up."

I can almost picture the two of them abusing some car they have absolutely no intention of buying, talking a bunch of trash in the process, and making themselves complete pains in ass. It does seem fitting.

"Well that's two for two my friend." I raise my bottle of beer.

His bottle meets mine halfway across the table, and we tap them lightly together as he keeps working that wonderful smile.

"I thought you might like that one."

Chapter 16

It's been only three days since I last saw her, but the more I sit here thinking about it, the more it feels like it's been an eternity.

She called me at work earlier to tell me how much she missed me, and said she thought there was a good chance she could sneak away tonight for a couple of hours. Dave has to attend some sort of a business dinner, and if everything goes according to plan, she's going to tell him that she's heading to the mall to do some shopping.

So here I sit on my sofa at a little after seven on Tuesday evening, biding my time about as patiently as a young child waiting to open Christmas presents. I'm unable to concentrate on anything other than seeing her again. Remaining ever hopeful, I take yet another look at my watch. She had figured on being here no later than seven.

I'm not even in the mood to eat dinner, and I can't remember the last time that happened. Probably when I had that serious bout with the flu.

I left the Tahoe in the driveway and the garage door open so she could pull right in. I need to program one of the buttons in her car so she can open it by remote next time. The television's off and the stereo's on standby. I'll start the background music once I know she's here, but in the mean time I'm not in the mood to listen to it. I'd rather wait in silence.

One thing I know for sure, I won't be able to continue like this for very long. It's not in my nature to be sneaking around with someone, and I can't stand the idea of her having to go home every night to an abusive husband she despises. The thought of him groping at her body without invitation flashes through my mind, and if he were here right now, I'd be hard pressed not to beat him unconscious. On the other hand, I know I'm being naïve to think it hasn't happened at least once since I last saw her, and that as long as they're living together, it will continue to happen. The cold reality of it makes me furious.

I couldn't guess how many times I've wrestled with the sanity of what I'm involved in here. I would never have believed it possible until it happened. But then again, I am a firm believer in giving destiny its due, and there is no denying I have never wanted anyone more than I want her right now. I keep telling myself that what I'm feeling can't be love. It's too soon for that. It's probably nothing more than lustful infatuation. But regardless of what it is, I'm already in way too deep anyway, and only the test of time can render the final verdict. Besides, it's not as if the world isn't already full of unhappy couples having extramarital affairs. I'm not exactly pioneering new frontier here. I just wish I could make this guy go away, quickly and quietly.

I hear the sound of an approaching engine, becoming more of a rumble as it enters the garage.

Starting the music, I head for the inner door, as the stress that was tormenting me only seconds ago is immediately replaced with the excitement of seeing her, and the thrill of us once again making love.

"Hello there stranger." I say as she steps through the door and kisses me. I'm trying hard not to reveal how anxious I've become.

"Sorry I'm late sweetheart," her voice is soft and apologetic. The sound of her calling me sweetheart sends a tingle through my body. "But I wanted to buy something special for you."

"Oh?"

She smiles as she holds up a medium sized shopping bag. I recognize the name of the store immediately, and it's all I can do to maintain my composure. *Intimate Moments* is the same place Gina used to buy her most seductive lingerie.

"Any chance you're a fan of naughty looking lingerie?" she asks sweetly.

The smile I have on my face feels like it's running from ear to ear, and visions of what she might be wearing for me shortly begin to flash through my mind.

"You have no idea."

I wrap my arms around her, and we begin to kiss each other. Softly at first, gradually becoming more urgent. But then I slow it down, not wanting to go too far until I give her a chance to change. As if on cue, she backs away slightly.

"I just need a couple of minutes. Okay? It's been a long time since I've worn these kinds of things, and it took me awhile to get the garter straps right in the store earlier."

The thought of garter straps and what normally goes with them is driving me wild. They're always attached to something very sexy, and it also means that stockings are part of the package. I can't wait to see her wearing whatever it is.

"I'd be more than happy to help," I offer hopefully.

She playfully waves her finger at me in a scolding motion.

"You be a good boy, and promise not to peek until I'm ready."

Chapter 17

"Got a minute?"

I'm sitting at my desk on Thursday afternoon, signing checks to suppliers. Vinny or I sign every payment that leaves the company, and I try to do it personally as often as possible. There's no better way to make sure you stay in tune with where the money goes.

I look up to see him standing at the door, his right hand resting against the jamb. He looks a bit unhappy.

"Hey Chenz. What do you got?"

"The twins just called me after paying Preston a visit. You'll never guess who they ran into after taking Dave and one of his cars out for test spin."

Even though he doesn't really expect me to guess, I make the gesture to let him know I'm ready for the answer.

"Ruben Sanchez." His voice has an edge to it, which is understandable. It's a name I haven't heard in awhile, but one not easily forgotten.

"Ruben Sanchez? Wow! I haven't run into that nut job since trade school."

"Me either."

"Hey, remember the time he called you out?"

"Yes I do."

Ruben was a renowned bad ass in his own right, coming from a neighboring town called Brentwood, just northeast of Bay Shore. In his neck of the woods, nobody would dare mess with him. He wasn't Vinny's equal as a fighter, but he was closer than anyone else in school, and he also had a couple of screws loose to go along with it. That combination made him a dangerous person to tangle with, no matter who you were.

It evidently bothered him to no end that Vinny was so revered, and one day he figured it was time for him to prove he was top dog. To make a long story short, Ruben got his ass kicked, and Vinny had to keep a watchful eye on the guy for the rest of our senior year. He figured revenge was imminent at some point, but nothing ever came of it. Ruben must have concluded he was better off leaving well enough alone.

"So what was *he* doing there?"

"I'm not sure, but it seems that he's somehow involved in Dave's business."

"How's that?"

He can't hold back a smile as he gets ready to tell me.

"No sooner did the twins come to a screeching stop in front of Preston's showroom, when Ruben appeared out of nowhere, reached into the open driver's side window, and yanked Joe right through it and out of the car!"

Now I smile too at the thought of what Joe's expression must have looked like.

"Ruben never did like the twins, did he?"

"No, he didn't... And it seems he took that opportunity to make sure they understood things haven't changed."

"I hope he didn't get too nasty."

All joking aside, they were up there on my account, and I would feel responsible for anything bad that might have come from it.

His look turns serious. "No... But to save their necks, they wound up telling him and Dave that they were there on my behalf, sort of scouting out a car for me."

"You think they bought it?" I smile at myself for letting such a stupid question escape from my lips.

"Not very likely. And I'm sure it won't take too long for them to figure out the whole charade leads back to you."

"Yeah, you're right. And it's not what I need right now, but what are you going to do? It is what it is. So what's the short version of how it ended?"

"Ruben said to tell me to start shopping for my cars someplace else, and that if he ever catches the two of them there again, he won't be so friendly next time."

I wonder what in God's name Ruben could be up to with Dave Preston... and whether it makes the overall situation better or worse. At the moment, it's hard to imagine how it could make things any better.

"One thing they did find out," he interrupts my thoughts, "is that Dave appears to be running a chop shop in his auto body garage."

Now that might very well explain Ruben. From what little I have heard about him since our school days, he's evidently been involved in a number of illegal business ventures.

"How'd they do that?"

"They were snooping around the property when they first got there, and wandered into a large Quonset hut located well behind the main building. A side door was unlocked and they got a good look at a number of late model luxury cars in various stages of being torn apart. But it didn't take long for a couple of goons to appear, finding it hard to believe they got lost while looking for the showroom, and the goons threatened to beat the hell out of them if they ever "got lost" there again."

Those two are like a pathetic version of the Hardy Boys, but they just might have stumbled onto something worthwhile.

"I haven't heard from Peter Long yet, but I'll be very surprised if he comes up with anything on the Ruben connection."

"I agree," he nods his head.

"Any ideas on how we might find out?"

"Yeah... I'll bet Fat Tony knows. He tends to travel in those circles."

"I was afraid you were going to say that, but you're probably right. Is he still talking to us?"

"Not really. But I'm sure he'll be happy to if I ease up some on our credit terms."

Fat Tony. What a freaking lowlife. Unfortunately, right now I may have to be nice to him.

"Okay Chenz, see what you can find out, and do whatever you think is fair. But don't give him a nickel more than you have to."

Chapter 18

Memorial Day begins the peak season for those who frequent Fire Island, but with school out and summer in full swing, the Fourth of July is always a much bigger event.

"All aboard! Last call... Fair Harbor and Dunewood!" I hear the young mate on the dock yell as loud as he can, almost overtaxing his adolescent voice and screwing up an otherwise suitable sound of authority. The ferry is packed, and the hot morning air is charged with excitement over the weekend to come. Every face I look at is smiling or doing something close to it. Chatter is coming from all directions, and it's easy to hear some of the big plans being made for the next few days. Most of the youngsters are boisterous and misbehaving more than usual, but the general mood of the adults is so cheerful that it seems to balance things out, and make it feel more acceptable. All in all it's a glorious Friday morning, and I wish I could be more joyful, but I'm feeling terribly hollow inside.

Sitting in the sunshine on the upper deck gives me a panoramic view of the surrounding neighborhood. A single aisle separates the bench seats on either side of it, and I've managed a seat on the inner end, right about amidships on the port side. I like having the freedom to get up and move whenever I feel like it, without having to bother anybody else.

This ferry leaves from the next canal east of my home, and looking straight ahead I can just make out a tiny piece of my property, barely visible in a gap between the buildings and vehicles that dot the parking lots of the two adjacent terminals. Looking south, the bay appears calm, and a number of boats are making their way in and out of the marina. One is idling patiently near the gas dock at the rear of the snack bar, waiting his turn to take on fuel. Considering the holiday, I'm surprised there's not more of a line, but with the recent spike in oil prices it's becoming a harder luxury for many to afford.

The captain enters the small pilothouse and fires up the engines one at a time, then signals the crew to release the lines. Latecomers search for a place to sit as we start to back slowly away from the pier.

With this particular weekend upon us, there's almost no chance at all that Atlantique still has a single slip open of any size. Vinny and I brought our boats over after work on Wednesday afternoon and left them there, taking an evening ferry home from Dunewood. It's technically against the rules of Atlantique to leave your boat there unattended, but everybody does it anyway. George Brenner called me from there yesterday morning and told me it was a good thing we did, because all of the larger slips were taken by ten A.M., and it didn't appear that anyone was budging until Monday afternoon.

I was going to bring the Whaler over this morning, but Vinny's coming later in the day with some provisions, and I figured it would be a lot easier for him if he used it for that. He's sending one of the boys from the shop to pick up the steaks I ordered from the butcher, and then down to the seafood store to grab some live lobsters for tonight. He's also bringing a couple of large coolers packed full of ice to top off the ones already on the boats. At least from the standpoint of food and refreshments we'll be in great shape for the entire weekend. I only wish I could say the same for my love life.

I've spoken to Jill so many times since we were together on Tuesday that I can't remember them all. I gave her a cell phone to make it easier for her to call me, and it seems we've been talking for a good part of every day since. I can't get enough of it though, and I'm amazed at how the simple sound of someone's voice can stir such deep and passionate emotions. Even right now, I'm unable to think about anything else. Add to that, the memory of how inviting and playful she looked dressed in that naughty looking lingerie, teasing and pleasing me so lovingly, completely immersed in wanting to make me happy.

It's killing me not to have her here by my side.

Dave took their boat over yesterday morning and left it there as well. They're taking the noon ferry out of the Bay Shore Marina in a couple of hours, going directly into Atlantique. It's bound to be pure torture seeing each other from a distance all weekend long, likely not getting the chance to say much more than hello. The thought even crossed my mind last night to retrieve my boat and head off somewhere else for the holiday to avoid the agony, but I'm sure it would be far worse to not see her at all. At least I'll know where she is and that she's all right.

During our conversation earlier this morning, she told me she's finally come up with an idea of how to rid herself of Dave without recourse, but she won't tell me what it is until the next time we're alone. This, I can't wait to hear, because at the rate I'm going, I'm about to bust a mental gasket. Something has got to be done with this guy, and it needs to happen sometime soon.

According to Peter Long, he's a financial time bomb ready to blow. The guy is in debt up to his ears with a hefty mortgage on everything he owns. Couple that with what Fat Tony told Chenz, and he's a complete disaster. The word is, he's into Ruben for two hundred large from gambling losses, and because he's unable to make his payments on time, he's been forced into chopping stolen cars. Knowing Ruben to the extent that I do, I'm sure the alternative choice was having a number of bones broken... or worse. Too bad Ruben offered him an option.

Now this is an angle I need to keep in mind, although the thought of doing business with Ruben is a very unpleasant one. I'm also sure he could never be trusted to keep a secret. In fact, thinking about it some more, being part of something criminal with that guy would almost certainly lead to being blackmailed.

Those are the kind of opportunities I'll bet he lives for, leveraging other people's misery in any way he can to make a buck. Especially when he knows the victim has a lot more to lose than he does.

The thing that scares me the most, is that a guy like Dave, who is already prone to violence, will snap at some point and go off the deep end. And when that happens, Jill's the most likely candidate to be on the receiving end of his wrath. If he decides to do something irrational, I'm sure he'll want to have her along for the ride. He's not the kind of guy who'd sacrifice his own welfare for her future happiness with someone else.

Knowing what I know now, I'm even more thankful she accepted the money I gave her on Tuesday. She used her secret stash to spring for the lingerie, and only after considerable prodding did she admit there wasn't much of it left. Not only was the use of a credit card out of the question due to the obvious trail it would leave, but she told me Dave watches her like a hawk when it comes to spending a dime. It seems he does more than enough of that for both of them.

She deserves a lot better, and I plan on being the person who gives it to her. I smile at the thought of how much she appreciated the gift after getting over her initial embarrassment. I think seeing a thousand in cash was a real surprise, and it deeply touched her. The look on her face was priceless.

Hearing the engines begin to race and the boat accelerate, I look up as we break the mouth of the marina and head for the first channel marker. I was so preoccupied in my thoughts that I hardly realized where we were until I heard the sound.

The bay is calm, and the fresh salt air is invigorating. In spite of my excessive despair, I need to keep the right perspective on things, and never forget how fortunate I am.

What a beautiful morning it is to be alive, healthy, and heading to the beach.

•

Chapter 19

Fair Harbor is one town further west from Atlantique than Dunewood, but I forgot my newspaper at the shop, and Dunewood doesn't have a market. It's also a nice morning to enjoy the longer journey.

More than half the passengers pour from the ferry here, momentarily challenging the capacity of the pier where friends and family wait to greet them. It's almost gridlock as the cheerful crowd exchanges long hellos, but I manage to steadily prod my way through the masses.

I'm in the heart of the tiny town as soon as I step from the ferry landing. The whole commercial area consists of a few old single story wood structures forming a small corner on the main walk along the bay. A storage rack full of little red wagons and a busy bicycle stand are both testaments to this being a family community. I contemplate stopping at the hardware store, as I often do, to browse the wares and enjoy the atmosphere more reminiscent of a general store, but I can't think of anything I need right now and I decide to skip it this time. Newspapers are stacked outside of the market as usual, and I grab both a Newsday and Times on my way inside to pay.

As is true with every store on the island that I'm familiar with, there's nothing overly fancy about this place. But, it has a special feeling to it that you want to be a part of. It always makes me think of simpler times. Heavily worn wooden floors, a couple of antiquated manual checkout counters, and a wall of open refrigerated display cases from another generation. The kind with clear plastic straps that hang between you and the food to keep the cold air inside. It's clean and well stocked, though, offering the fresh breads, produce, and deli foods that affluent people are happy to pay a premium for this far from home.

When the weather cooperates, they do some terrific business here, and I'll bet the owner makes a fairly decent living for only seasonal work. On the other hand, I'm sure that a summer full of rainy weekends can quickly test the strength of his bank account, and possibly even challenge his fortitude to stay the course another year.

I grab a cold bottle of apple juice, and finish it before a young dad and his daughter in front of me clear the register. She looks to be about five or six years old, and he couldn't be older than his late twenties. She's as cute as a doll, standing barely as high as his waist, having to reach almost straight up to hold his hand. Purple flip-flops contrast a tiny yellow bathing suit, and brown pigtails frame the sides of her pink Mini Mouse sunglasses. She's noticeably happy to be with her dad, and it touches me to see how she looks at him as he hands her the candy bar she wanted.

"Thank you daddy!" she smiles cheerfully, standing on tippy toes to give him a kiss. He bends down to embrace her briefly as they start for the exit a few feet away. He has this big smile on his face, and I find myself envious of how special he must be feeling right now. The love of your own flesh and blood must be an amazing thing to experience.

It warms my heart to see the teenage checkout girl make correct change without a machine to help her, and I gladly accept the plastic bag she offers for my newspapers. Back outside in the sunshine, I notice the ferry mob heading my way. If I loiter too long I'll be dodging my way around wagons, kids, and coolers again. Failing to catch another glimpse of the little girl and her dad, I turn inland to begin my trek. I guess they headed towards the bay, somewhere lost in the bustling crowd. No doubt bringing a smile to the face of any elder remembering similar times with their own children.

Tall dense thicket lines either side of the cement walk beginning only a few steps from the market, and whatever breeze existed near the bay diminishes quickly. But it also brings some shade to offset the growing heat of the sun, and I settle into a comfortable pace as my mind becomes preoccupied with thoughts of having my own family.

The gentle ring of a bicycle bell warns me of one approaching from the rear, and I move to the right as an elderly lady slowly peddles by. Like many you see over here, the bike is an old single speed, half rusted away. It's a fitting background against the aged and leathery tanned legs that propel it without shoes. Her gray scraggly hair is gathered behind her head, falling slightly onto a plain white tee shirt. I notice the bike sway a little with each pump of the pedals, at first suggesting a lack of sufficient energy to control the thing. But I see the routine continue consistently around two other people up ahead of me, and it now appears to be more of an off beat steady rhythm. Something she can probably do for a good part of the day if she puts her mind to it.

I make a left on the main walkway running east to west. It's made of cement in this area, and wide enough to support about twice as much foot traffic as the narrow walks that intersect it from north to south. A young mother with two youngsters is crossing up ahead on the way to the ocean, heavily burdened with all sorts of beach paraphernalia. I smile as I try to picture Jill doing that in a few years. What a pleasant thought - Jill being the mother of my children.

It's not too long before I'm passing the tennis courts of Dunewood, and as often happens by the time I reach this spot, I've become the lone pedestrian. In another minute or so, I'm at the far end of town, where cement pavement turns abruptly to a winding road of deep, unruly sand. You can trudge it all the way to Ocean Beach if you're so inclined, but it takes a strong spirit of adventure and a lot of stamina, not to mention a good dose of sunscreen. It's much better suited for the four-wheel drives that occasionally traverse this island during the off-season, than it is for foot traffic. Gina and Roseanne used to joke that they once ran into a camel on the sweltering sand of that road somewhere east of Atlantique. I think if they hadn't laughed so much when they told the story, I might have even believed them.

I duck under the branches of a tree partially blocking a small wooden walk that looks less than inviting. It's enough to suggest to the uninformed that they're risking a fate worse than the sudden transition of the main road. In reality, it's a considerably shorter route with an abundance of shade that's much easier on the legs.

Some of the homes along this stretch of secluded walk barely qualify as inhabitable, at least in my opinion. They're little more than run down shacks occupying a low-lying area that's swampy most of the time, with all of them connected by a maze of elevated boardwalks so narrow that two people can hardly walk side by side. But there never seems to be a problem finding some Manhattanite anxious to rent such modest dwellings for the summer. I guess only the lure of sand and ocean can make people willingly pay so handsomely to indulge such challenging accommodations.

I don't hear any air conditioners running, and many of the scattered window screens are in disrepair. I can't imagine what it must be like to be around here when dusk arrives. I'll bet the mosquitoes have a regular field day.

Several turns later I'm back on solid pavement, the homes here rather grand in comparison to those I left behind in the scrubland. These are the ones I usually think of when I'm picturing a beach house in my mind. They're modest structures, but clean and freshly painted, with pieces of driftwood scattered on the sandy lawns of clumpy crabgrass, and wild bamboo giving privacy to decks and property lines. An unseen wind chime is making soft lazy music somewhere close by. The house coming up on my left has two wicker rocking chairs resting on a small covered porch. An old wooden rowboat is half buried in the middle of the front yard serving as a planter. Nice touch.

"Daddy called!" I hear a woman's voice somewhere off to my right. "He's coming over on the next ferry!"

It sounds like at least four children are happily cheering the news. What a feeling it must be to have kids that love you so much. I hope some day I'm that fortunate. Had Gina and I still been together, that could have been us by now. We talked about having children all the time, and who knows, maybe if we had just done it rather than procrastinate over the timing, we would still be together. I shake that thought, replacing it quickly with one of Jill and I making love - the thought of her and I having children together.

Two blocks later I leave the pavement for the final time, stepping down onto a grassy road that leads into the west side of Atlantique. Dense weeds are once again lining the way, but there's a sliver of blue up ahead where the path ends on the bayside beach of the marina. I can already hear the sounds of activity; a parent warning a young one not to venture too far into the water, someone named Bobby being told to play nice and share his toys, a cook announcing loudly that his hot dogs and hamburgers are ready.

I'm halfway across the sand running between the beach and the playground when I notice *Second Time Around* on the west dock. It looks to be exactly where it was when we had our first encounter. Vinny's on the south side of it this time, and I'm on the west side of the south dock, close to where I was then as well. This should all make for a very interesting and unpleasant weekend - the thought of her being alone with him on that boat is enough to make me sick. I hope that whatever her plan is, she intends to act on it soon.

Chapter 20

"Look, Debbie, I appreciate the thought, but I'm really not interested."

"Oh Michael, believe me, she's a doll. You know I wouldn't try to set you up with anyone I didn't think the world of. Why don't you just let her come over on the ferry tomorrow morning and I'll make sure she goes back on the three o'clock. I'll tell her you already have plans for the evening. No pressure at all from me once you meet her, I promise."

Debbie doesn't have a clue yet about Jill, and I want to make sure it stays that way for now. She came over with Vinny on the Whaler a couple of hours ago, and the three of us are sitting in the cockpit of my boat having cocktails. I look over at Vinny for help.

"Deb, what Michael is trying to tell you nicely is that he doesn't want any part of whatever it is you have in mind. So just let it go."

His tone is on the firm side, and I can see she's hurt. She attempts to smile her understanding, but it's obviously a forced gesture. I feel bad, but at the same time, I don't like having to say *no* over and over again.

"Maybe some other time... Okay?" I offer consolingly.

"Okay Michael. You win." She smiles more naturally as she takes a sip of her wine.

Looking away for a moment, I glimpse a rather large group making their way slowly down the busy afternoon dock. Sure enough, it's the Preston's and their visiting entourage. They passed the boat earlier heading to the ocean, two of Dave's buddies boasting about how many beers they were able to cram into the cooler they were carrying. Jill managed a brief smile in my direction, but that was about it. Torture. From what she told me, these guys all work for Dave, nothing close to being genuine friends. She gets along well enough with the girls, but since she's the boss's wife she'll never have more than a superficial relationship with any of them. And, there's not a happy marriage among the lot.

Dave's in the lead as usual, and I see him nudging the big guy next to him, like an overgrown juvenile delinquent in the process of scheming trouble. He's as easy to read as a book.

"Asshole alert." I say it just loud enough for Vinny to hear me.

"Hey!" Dave barely reaches the boat when he starts to speak, "I forgot to tell you guys something earlier… an old friend of yours wanted me to say hello."

He stops right in front of us, a wiseass grin spread across his face. The girls appear to want no part of it, and they continue on their way.

"Yeah..." He pauses with a more serious look. No doubt trying to be overly dramatic, but a stupid looking grin reappears almost immediately. I'll bet he can't tell a good joke to save his life.

"Ruben Sanchez sends his *personal* regards." He announces it like an important news flash.

What a shocking surprise.

He's nudging the guy next to him again, and the two boys right behind them are both smiling along. As if their association with Ruben has somehow elevated their stature in life.

"Ruben Sanchez? You guys know Ruben?" I make it sound like I'm surprised and impressed. Their smiles are growing. "Hey Chenz. You remember Ruben, don't you?"

"Of course I do," Vinny starts smiling too. "How could I ever forget Ruben Sanchez? Hey... would you guys mind doing me a favor?"

Four heads are now shaking in the affirmative, all thrilled to death that playing the Ruben card has softened us up so quickly.

"Well the next time you guys are all sitting around and chewing the fat with your good buddy Ruben..."

He pauses for effect, chuckling lightheartedly, as if he's recollecting something they'll find mutually amusing - possibly a lighter side to someone as nasty and menacing as Ruben - and talk about hook, line, and sinker, his audience is riveted.

"You have just got to make him tell you about the time, back when we went to school together…"

They're all nodding faster, trying to speed him.

"When he pissed me off one day… And I… I kicked the shit out of him!"

He turns to me. "You remember that, don't you Michael?"

"Yeah. That was pretty funny," I agree, the smile fading from my face. I stare straight into Dave's eyes to make sure he knows how serious I am.

"That guy was always such a *pussy*," Vinny adds for good measure, making it sound like the very thought of Ruben is repulsive.

No one is smiling anymore, and it only takes Dave a split second to start looking angry and foolish. But I sense vengeance more than intimidation in his eyes, and as I recall Jill's warning, I swear I can almost see the demented wheels of his brain racing in fast-forward. He turns to leave without saying another word, and three sullen faces follow right after him… shoulders slumped, and chins a lot closer to their chests now. Even the cooler hanging between the arms of the two guys bringing up the rear is sagging noticeably lower than it was before.

"What was that all about?" Debbie wants to know.

"Oh, nothing really. It was just a *guy* thing," Vinny tells her, having no intentions of explaining the Ruben connection. "You wouldn't understand."

"How can you be so sure?"

"Because I am. It's the whole Mars and Venus thing. You know, there are certain things we do that you will never understand, no matter how hard you try... and vice versa."

"So come on, try me anyway."

He looks slightly annoyed for a second, but then appears to gather a thought.

"Okay... It's sort of like the way us guys go around, jumping up and trying to touch stuff all the time."

"What?"

"I'm just giving you an example. Can you ever remember seeing a group of young women passing under a doorway, all jumping up, trying their best to slap the overhead jamb as they go? Seeing who can, and who can't do it? Of course not - because girls don't do that. They don't get it. Now you see what I mean?"

She's staring at him with a flustered look. "Forget I asked."

Chapter 21

There's no moon at all tonight, and the darkness of the beach is so thick that after almost twenty minutes of adjustment I'm still struggling to see much of anything. The ocean waves are pounding not far away, but I can't tell where the surf line is. Thankfully a warm pleasant breeze is blowing most of the mist out to sea. Even with that, the cool frothy smell of the ocean water permeates the air.

Once again I scan the end of the dimly lit walkway leading from the marina, and there's still no sign of her. I'm sure she said midnight sharp, and it has to be at least ten minutes after. My back is close to the stick wire fence guarding the dunes, and I'm holding my knees close to my stomach as I sit and wait on the blanket spread beneath me. The landing of the walkway is no more than forty yards away, but there's no way anyone standing there could look into the darkness and see me. It was the perfect place to suggest such a rendezvous, and all I have to hope for now is that it happens. I'm desperately yearning for the chance to make love to her again. The feel of her creamy smooth skin against mine, the energy of our bodies pouring feverishly into one another. Hearing her tell me in the moment of passion how she needs me even more than I need her.

It seems Dave didn't take our afternoon exchange very well, and wound up pretty trashed before the sun went down. That man definitely has issues. Jill called me around ten and figured at the rate he was going he ought to be out like a light before eleven. Now I'm getting concerned that maybe he caught her sneaking out and things got ugly. I'm tempted to pay them a visit and make sure she's all right, but I know at this stage of the game it would only make matters worse.

I look again, about to give up, staring intently now at the sparse beam of light coming from the short solitary lamp pole near the end of the landing. It's engulfed by darkness only a few feet away. The better part of a minute must go by before a shadow finally emerges from the night, a lone thin figure with an unmistakable stride. My pulse quickens with excitement as I watch her pass under the lamp, stepping down to the sand and starting towards where she knows I'm waiting.

"Over here!" I call as loudly as I dare, standing up and moving towards her. It seems like forever since we last held each other.

Without a word being spoken, my hand receives hers. We kiss urgently as I lift her into my arms, bringing her over to the blanket and carefully laying her down. We continue to kiss as I straddle her legs, our tongues now searching hungrily for affection, quickly reaching an understanding that there will be no foreplay tonight. Her fingers tug sharply against the waist of my bathing suit; I lean backwards, removing my shirt as she strips the suit from my legs, and then she pushes me gently onto the flat of my back. I can barely see her breasts as she stands above me removing her bra, and there is only the slightest hint of pubic hair between her legs as she steps from her light colored panties. It's now she who straddles me, her right hand pressing firmly against my chest as she lowers herself to kiss me, the left one guiding my painfully stiff erection into her wet wondrous warmth.

Chapter 22

"*Kill him? That's the best you can come up with? Are you serious?*"

So much for the magic I was feeling right after we came together. I'm waiting for the laughter to start, the kind that normally follows somebody being totally faked out, like I'm hoping I was a second ago. Not that I'm often guilty of being so gullible, or that I enjoy the experience, but I wouldn't mind a good laugh right now at my expense.

"I'm dead serious!" she whispers adamantly, lying alongside me now on the blanket with her head resting against my chest, an arm across my stomach.

Wow! She's not kidding. I honestly didn't have a clue what to expect, but I know it wasn't this.

"*Jill*, listen to me. Please. We'll figure out something else. I promise."

She starts to cry.

"I can't do this anymore Michael. It's awful!" Now it turns more to sobbing. "It was bad enough before I met you, and now it's intolerable. I have to do something soon."

She catches half a breath.

"Every time he touches me, I want to scream out your name, tell him that I belong to you now, and to keep his filthy hands off me. I can't believe I ever married such an animal, that I was once intimate with him."

I feel like screaming out myself at the thought of him touching her. Husband or not, no one has the right to touch someone else that doesn't want to be touched.

"I love you Jill... and it's killing me to not have you with me all the time, but there's got to be a better way to deal with this guy. A way that doesn't wind up ruining your own life in the process."

"Then what is it?" her tone is now challenging.

"I don't know yet, but there has to be." My voice is also firm.

She doesn't reply right away. There's nothing but the sound of the surf for a minute or two, and then her hand once again begins stroking my stomach.

"Can I at least tell you my idea?" the tone is now soft and hopeful.

I really don't want to hear this, but I somehow find myself intrigued. "Okay... I'll listen. But don't expect me to agree with anything, and I mean that."

Her head nods against my chest. Then I feel the warmth of her leg sliding along the top of mine as she moves up into a more comfortable position to talk.

"Well you see... Dave's uncle has this vacation cabin upstate in the middle of nowhere. Nothing else around it but state owned land for miles. We used to go there once in awhile when we first got married, and he's always nagging me about going back again. He wants to spend a weekend there together. Just the two of us."

I'm already not liking the sound of this, but I keep my mouth shut.

"The property borders on a big lake, and his uncle has a power boat that he keeps moored at a small finger dock he built. Other than that, there's nothing but pine trees and dense growth surrounding the rest of the lake. His uncle uses the boat mostly for fishing, but Dave and his cousins use it more for water skiing and horsing around."

"Must be a relaxing place."

"It could be, but not when you're there with the wrong person."

"Yeah. I know what you mean." It sounds like boating with Allison.

"Anyway… one drink that Dave will never put to his lips is rum. He got really sick from drinking a whole bottle of it years ago, and now he can't even handle the smell."

What a coincidence. I had a similar experience with that stuff myself.

"In case you haven't noticed, Dave drinks more than enough when he drinks alone. And when I'm sometimes in the mood to have a couple of drinks with him, he usually drinks to excess… So what I plan on doing, is buying a bottle of rum and dumping most of it out. Then I'll fill it back up with water, and get Dave to think I'm in the mood to party."

Now she's starting to scare me. "Doesn't he always get nasty when he drinks?"

"Up to a point. But when he gets totally shit faced, he tends to be a happy drunk. Especially when I'm drinking with him. If I'm having a few myself, and not giving him grief over it, he's a whole lot easier to get along with."

"So you get him drunk as a skunk. He's happy. Then what?" I hope this is getting better in a hurry.

"I get him to take me for a boat ride."

"A boat ride?"

"Yeah, a boat ride… And once we're out on the lake, I'll happen to lose my hat or something overboard, so he'll have to stop and go back for it. Then, when he's leaning over the side to pick it up… I'll push his sorry ass into the lake."

"Hoping for what, that he'll drown?"

This sounds like one hell of a long shot.

"No. It wouldn't be easy to convince anyone who knows him that he managed to drown by accident. He's a good swimmer, and even drunk he could probably make it to shore from anywhere on the lake."

"So?"

"So… I'm going to run him over with the boat and kill him!"

She certainly said that like she meant it.

"Run him over? Won't that be even more obvious?"

"No. Not the way I plan on doing it. It will definitely appear to be an accident, a very tragic one at that. After I'm sure he's under for good, I'll bring the boat back towards the cabin, passing close to the dock while I'm making a fairly sharp turn. Then I'll jump off and swim for shore, letting the boat run aimlessly in circles until it hits the shore somewhere; just like it would if a drunk reckless driver fell overboard while horsing around."

"Run over by his own boat?" I'm trying to make it sound like a far-fetched idea, not giving it too much credence. But the more I think about it, the more I have to admit, it has the makings of a perfect crime. It's pretty clever.

"I'll wash and dry my clothes, taking my time to make sure I don't forget to clean anything up," she continues calmly, "then I'll call the police and report the terrible news… He was drinking heavily as he's known to do, we had one of our usual arguments, and he headed for the boat in a tizzy to blow off some steam. It was only after he was gone much longer than usual that I started to worry, and that's when I went outside and noticed the empty boat had run ashore, my poor husband nowhere to be seen."

Am I totally losing my mind? I'm listening to a murder plan that I'm part of by association, and I'm finding myself impressed. How has such craziness made its way into my otherwise rational life in the course of only a couple of weeks? Then again, why do I ask myself such questions? I know exactly how it happened. This woman is all I can think about day and night, the soul mate I had all but given up hope for. So sweet and caring, yet possessing enough spirit to fight for keeps when she's been pushed too far. I can relate to that... maybe not the actual killing part of it, but certainly the instinct to retaliate when I've had all I can take from someone... and it somehow touches me deeply to know I'm part of the reason she's looking to do it. Truth be known, I've already thought about killing this guy more than once on my own - or, at least having him killed. Reality is though, even the best laid plans are a roll of the dice, and the downside scenario here is extremely unattractive. Even as an accomplice there's a hell of a lot to lose, and that's assuming I could let her go it alone, which I seriously doubt.

I have no intention of chasing a dream, no matter how amazing it may be, only to find myself in jail for the rest of my life; or worse. I'd be sacrificing everything I've worked so hard for, and likely coming up on the short end of the stick anyway. This is *nuts*.

I've got to convince her that one way or another, murder is not the answer.

Chapter 23

Stepping from the comfort of the cabin, my bare feet grudgingly make their way across the cold morning dew that covers the cockpit deck. I saw the cell phone from the salon window, lying by itself on the small table next to the transom door. It looks like there's a note wrapped around it held by a rubber band.

It's not quite six o'clock yet, and the marina's socked in by a thick blanket of fog. I can't see halfway down the dock. It's a complete, eerie calm, and if anyone else is stirring, they're doing it very quietly. I pick up the phone and head back inside. The bottom of it's dry, so it's been there for a while. I don't have a good feeling about this. I still can't believe how quickly things unraveled last night; how upset she got when I tried to make her promise she wouldn't do anything rash.

At first I'm tempted to bide my time, so I place it on the countertop, figuring there's no reason to rush into reading bad news. I grab the coffee from the refrigerator and a filter from the cabinet over the stove, but my willpower disintegrates before I pour the water. I reach instead for the note, unfolding it carefully, almost afraid to read what it says, but I have to know.

Dear Michael,

As much as I love you, I now realize it was wrong to involve you. Please forgive me. It's not your problem and I had no right to make you feel like it was. I will never in my life forget you and the happiness you made me feel. It's more than I could have ever dreamed possible. You're such a good man and you deserve better than me. I sincerely hope you someday find your special someone.

Love always,

Jill

The full gravity of it hits me right away and I'm suddenly feeling ill. She's flat out dumping me, just like that, without any further conversation. Everything we had talked about together, our entire future, to her, is now meaningless. Oh, she was very nice about it, but it's nevertheless the same result. She knew the cell phone was the only means I had to get in touch with her, so she has intentionally made it impossible for me to reach her. I read the note over and over again, desperately trying to make sense of it.

Chapter 24

After getting over my initial shock and despair, I'm feeling more anger than anything else. Soul mates? What a joke. One argument and she calls it quits. Granted, the subject matter wasn't trivial, but it was still the only argument we've had, and she wouldn't even give round two a chance. So much for my lousy intuition, I was so sure she was heaven sent.

My first thought was to pack up and get away from this place. Go off and anchor somewhere in privacy to lick my wounds. But I'm not going anywhere. I'm doing my best to enjoy the rest of this weekend in spite of what happened. I'm even thinking about having Debbie call her girl friend.

Putting things in perspective, all I am at the moment, is right back where I was a couple of weeks ago. Big deal. Was life so terrible then? No. Well, maybe not terrible, but I was awfully lonely; and I had definitely never felt anything like her before.

The thought of us making love on the beach last night hits me. The feel of us wanting each other so badly, our bodies thrusting in wild harmony, the final rush of pleasure, the overwhelming sensation of total satisfaction.

I've got this pit in my stomach now and it hurts like hell. I think I need a nice long jog on the beach.

Chapter 25

"I fold."

"You're *folding?* What are you Frank, some kind of a *moron?* In case you forgot, you're in the Big-Blind, and since nobody else raised you, it costs you absolutely nothing to see the flop."

"Oh yeah... I forgot... Okay. Then I'm going *all in*. I bet everything."

"*All in?* You were just going to fold!"

"What's the matter Joe? No balls?"

"No balls my ass Frank! You can't say you're going to fold, and then turn around and go all in. It doesn't even make any sense!"

"To me it does."

"Oh yeah? Okay. Then I call."

And I thought I was miserable earlier. Playing cards with the Carbone brothers can be downright painful. It's only the first hand of the game, and one of them is already about to lose all their chips. They told me this is called No Limit Texas Hold'Em, a version of poker that's supposedly become quite popular lately.

George Brenner drains the last half of his drink after hearing Joe call. He looks puzzled and just shakes his head. At the rate he's drinking, it's not going to get any better.

"I fold." He tosses his two cards face down on the table.

I grimace sarcastically at Vinny, wanting him to know how much I appreciate this brilliant idea of his to cheer me up. Not that I had any other bright ideas myself, and I have to admit these guys have been fairly amusing since they got here. I probably should have stuck to the original plan, though, which was to play on Vinny's boat so I could have bailed out quickly when I got tired of it. But my cockpit is much bigger, with a nice shaded area, and there's more of a breeze along the south dock. All in all, it's not a bad way to spend a Saturday afternoon. It certainly beats the hell out of the alternative, which was to sit around and sulk. Plus it's the first time I've ever seen the twins wearing bathing suits, and that's a refreshing change in itself... although, they could have made a better selection. They're real baggy blue ones, about two sizes too big, with worn out surfing slogans printed all over them. I noticed "surfs-up" and "hang-ten", but I was afraid to keep looking. I'll bet they ran out to buy them right after Vinny called this morning, and it never occurred to either one of them to choose different styles, much less colors. But at least they're wearing solid white T-shirts, with no first names or company logos.

"You guys play this game a lot?" I'm curious to know how long it took them to reach this level of skill.

"Believe it or not, we only started a few weeks ago," Joe answers. "We play with some of the boys in the shop at lunch time."

I don't know why that should surprise me, but it does.

"Must be good for employee relations," I say sarcastically.

"Hey, I heard you guys went up and made your peace with Lester," Vinny changes the subject.

"Yeah, I guess you could say that," Frank says with a smile. "You should have been there buddy, it was pretty funny."

"We got Lester into thinking we might buy another machine," Joe interrupts, "you know, to get him in a good mood and join us for dinner."

"Yeah, and after we got a few drinks in him we talked him into going to a strip joint, which as you probably know, isn't the kind of thing he normally likes to do. We had a few more drinks, a couple of lap dances, and the whole time we're there Joe and I are stuffing business cards and dollars bills into stockings and panties."

"It finally got to the point where his curiosity got the best of him," Joe says, "and he wanted to know what's up with the business cards. He couldn't believe we were *'sticking them in the undergarments of strange women in such a vile, sleazy place'*," he mimics the sound of Lester's more refined British voice as he finishes.

Frank slaps his knee as he bursts out laughing.

"That's when I tell him that the cards aren't ours, they're his! Joe took a stack of them off his desk earlier in the day!"

Laughter erupts uncontrollably now, with a booming roar from George making most of the racket, and he doesn't even know Lester.

"Oh man," Joe adds, "talk about going totally ballistic. He went nuts!"

One of these days they're going to push Lester too far, and then he's going to get real nasty. But for me to suggest anything in the way of caution would be a complete waste of my time.

Vinny decides to fold, and I join him. I have a pair of pocket nines, but it's too early in the game to risk losing everything to one of these maniacs.

"I got to tell you Michael," Frank leans back in his chair and looks unusually serious, "this is really the way to live. I have to hand it to you guys." He's looking up and down the dock, taking it all in. I think he just got a sense of what it's all about over here. "You know Joe, we ought to look into getting ourselves a boat."

That thought scares me. The next thing you know, they'll be over here every weekend or asking me to dock it at my house, and I could never put up with either part of that crap.

"It's an incredible drain on the bank account. I can tell you that much." I make it sound like friendly concern.

"Well it can't be any worse than working for Fat Tony," Joe says. "That guy's killing us."

"Hey, I told you two a long time ago to watch your ass when it came to Fat Tony," Vinny cuts in, "and all you keep doing is burying yourselves deeper and deeper. It's almost as if you enjoy the abuse."

"When you're right, you're right," Joe concedes. "You know what that prick came up with last week? He said that because he supplies us with the raw material we use to make his parts, he wants us to give him a *chip credit!* An immediate price reduction on every part we make for him, equal to the value of the scrap metal. As if we didn't understand the value of *that* when we originally quoted the work, and didn't already figure it into the prices we bid. He came over with a list of part numbers, showing the raw material weights, finished part weights, and the difference that he wants a credit for. Can you imagine that? The man is so financially desperate that he's trying to totally screw us?"

"So why didn't you tell him to go fuck himself!" I want to know.

"That's exactly what we're going to do," Frank leans forward, "but we thought we'd have a little fun with the big prick before we did it."

"Yeah," Joe jumps in, "we set him up really good this time."

"You know how he loves to stop at The Clipper for a few drinks after work on Fridays?" Frank pauses to make sure we can picture the setting. "Well, Joe and I hired this gorgeous looking blonde to wander in last night, acting like she was waiting for her boyfriend, but sitting close enough to Tony so that he couldn't help but start hitting on her."

"And we were sitting right there!" Joe can't help himself.

"So Tony starts buying her drinks," Frank continues, "telling her all about what a big shot he is, and she's pretending to be super impressed - you know, flattered that such a man would be spending his time on her, and making him think that she's getting more pissed by the minute at the guy who supposedly stood her up."

"They get real chummy after a couple of hours," Joe takes over, "but she tells him that she never sleeps with a man until she gets to know him a little, and Fat Tony winds up having to settle for a dinner date this coming Tuesday." He snorts more than laughs.

"And after that," Frank's getting excited, "I'm pretty sure they'll be having dinner again on Wednesday and Thursday too. And then..." he gives his brother a playful jab in the stomach... "If I don't miss my guess, after dinner on Thursday, they'll be heading for a motel. It's going to be Fat Tony's *lucky* night."

They both start laughing about as loud as I've ever heard them. I look over at Vinny and George, making sure I'm not the only one who missed the punch line, but they're as lost as I am.

"So what's so damn funny?" Vinny wants to know. "You're actually paying to get the guy laid?"

"No! No!" Frank is working hard to regain his composure. "*She* isn't really a *she!* Get it? She's really a *he!*"

"A transvestite!" Joe blurts it out.

Everyone loses it now, with the first gulp of George's new drink spraying uncontrollably from his mouth. I have to admit, this is very funny stuff. I also couldn't think of a more deserving victim. I just hope Tony doesn't wind up killing the poor guy when he finds out the big surprise.

"I hope you warned this guy, or whatever he is, about Tony's temper," Vinny says it first.

"Hey, this guy's a professional," Joe counters, "and we're paying him top dollar. That's his problem."

"Did you ever think that just maybe *she* is a *she*, and you're the ones being hustled?" I ask.

"What do you think we are, stupid? Frank made him show us."

We all start laughing again.

"Yeah, and let me tell you, he is *definitely* a he, and Fat Tony's going to freak out big time when he reaches down and finds the wrong number. But I told tranny-man that if he pulls this gig off successfully, and shows up at The Clipper again this Friday to rub Tony's nose in it, they'll be another grand in it for him. And you know what? He didn't seem very concerned about Tony after hearing that. He doesn't see that kind of cash too often."

"I sure hope you guys can make it down to The Clipper for the grand finale," Joe adds.

"We wouldn't miss it for the world." I have to remember never to piss these guys off too much. They're further out there than I could have imagined.

"Holy shit… Joe! You have *got* to check this out!" Frank's nodding down towards the Dock Master's shack, where the walk leads back from the beach.

Joe's mouth drops opens as he turns to look, and then I get this sick feeling that I know what's coming. I steal a glance trying not to seem too obvious, and sure enough, here she comes, wearing the same skimpy bathing suit she wore that day we spent alone at the inlet. Damn it! This makes me so mad. No sooner do I start enjoying myself, and now this. I'm feeling jealous beyond reason, and it makes me furious to see her charms on open display to the entire world, especially these two.

"Maah…doan!" it flows from Joe's mouth like natural reflex.

"Come on Joe, control yourself," Vinny tries to help me, "she's a married woman. Let's get the flop on the table for crying out load."

"Oh man…" Frank chimes in, "if I was married to something like that, I'd be all over her like a cheap suit, and I'm talking about every second of the day."

"All right guys, try not to embarrass me too much, will you?" I do my best to sound indifferent as I watch her walk by without looking in our direction.

It was one thing to see her wearing that scanty little suit when we were alone together, feeling as if it was for my eyes only. But seeing it here in public makes me feel like something very private we shared has been violated. This is awful. The twins are unable to take their eyes off her. If we were on Vinny's boat, I'd be leaving right about now. She's doing this on purpose! She knows damn well how its affecting me, making sure I don't forget what I'm missing out on, giving my guests a little something to drool over as I sit here and helplessly watch them. Way to go Jill. Terrific idea.

Maybe I better think about this for a minute so I don't jump to hasty conclusions. I'll take my time and go over it slowly. Let's see… she left me because I wouldn't sanction a murder plan, and now, without any further discussion or compromise, she's doling out some additional punishment. And she is fully aware, that for me, this is definitely very tough punishment. I poured my heart out to her about my feelings on behavior like this. She knows how much it bothers me to have other men gawking at her. How could she purposely try to hurt me so badly?

Well, as far as I'm concerned, she may have written a very sweet note to end our relationship, but this escapade is total bullshit. It's disgraceful.

Chapter 26

I hardly slept at all last night, and whenever I did manage to slip into the subconscious I was dreaming of Jill. It was really more like a nightmare, the same one over and over again. We were in between the sheets, playfully teasing each other. She was driving me out of my mind with the touch of her hands. But every time she started to kiss her way down along my stomach, the doorbell would ring, and that's when it became a nightmare. It was the Carbone brothers picking her up for a dinner date, both of them wearing their dirty shop uniforms. And as soon as she heard their voices, she lost all interest in me. The next thing I knew, I was helping her choose a dress to wear for them, something extra sheer and sexy, desperately doing whatever it took to keep her attention for every last second I could manage.

What a horrible way to wrestle with loneliness.

The twins wound up leaving before dinner yesterday, which was fine with me. I found the card game getting old and their company becoming more unappealing right after the Jill incident. It made for a long afternoon.

They saw her and Dave returning from the beach later on and wanted to know what *that* was all about. They were ribbing Vinny a little, figuring their visit to the car lot was somehow connected to her on his behalf. But Vinny told them they were wrong, that Dave had welshed on a bet, and that was why he wanted him checked out. I think they bought the story, but who knows? And at this point, I really don't give a damn whether they did anyway. What's the difference?

It's another hot, sunny morning at the beach, and the ferry dock is packed with boaters waiting for their guests to arrive. I still can't believe what a change of events took place in less than two days. Jill and I were making love on the beach late Friday night - I was so confident there would never again be anyone else in my life, and here I am on Sunday morning waiting for a blind date. Her name's Marla, and she's been one of Debbie's friends since high school.

It hasn't gone unnoticed by me that Debbie's been smiling non stop since I agreed to do this, and I'm beginning to worry she's a lot happier for Marla than she is for me. I hope this doesn't wind up being a disaster. I've never done something like this before and I'm still trying to figure out why I'm doing it now. Maybe this is what they refer to as being on the rebound, being totally mixed up and reaching for anything.

Vinny and Debbie are already squeezed in against my left side, and someone's pushing to pass me on the right, as if there's room up front being reserved just for them. I feel something slip into my right pocket, and I reach for the hand trying to pick it. Surprised to learn I'm too late for that, I quickly turn to see what I'm dealing with, but all I notice is long brown hair moving into the crowd ahead of me. I would know that head of hair anywhere. Reaching further into my pocket I feel a folded piece of paper.

I'm still looking at the back of her head when Jill suddenly turns to face me, scrunching her nose and pressing her lips together to form a warm, sorrowful expression. She then turns into the crowd again. Well I'll be damned… that sure looked friendly and apologetic… I just felt a wonderful tug at my heart.

But what am I getting excited over? After everything that's happened, how could she possibly make things right? What a lousy time to get a note like this. I'm beyond anxious to know what it says, but there's no way I can read it here.

"There she is!" Debbie's waving, "over here Marla!"

Marla inches towards us through the swarm of people, and Debbie reaches out to greet her as she finally arrives. They both extend their arms straight up in the air, once again calling each other's name, and then a quick hug follows.

"Marla, you know Vinny."

"Of course I do. Hi Vinny!"

She offers Vinny the side of her cheek, and he bends down to kiss it.

"Hi Marla."

She turns to me before Debbie gets the chance.

"And don't tell me, you must be Michael."

This one's as sharp as a tack.

"Hey, that's quite a guess." I catch Vinny smirking in the corner of my eye. "It's nice to meet you Marla."

"Likewise." Thankfully, she doesn't add *I'm sure*. It sounds annoying enough without it.

I hold out my hand to take hers, but she chooses instead to kiss me on the cheek. No sooner does she retreat from doing that when I notice Jill pushing by in the crowd, and she appears to give Marla a shot in the back. I think it was an elbow.

"Ugh!" She turns on Jill. "Hey, that hurt! Watch it will you!"

I don't think anyone else saw the hit.

Trying my best to allow for the fact she was struck rather hard by surprise, I still think that voice had a lot of *bitch* in it. Not that my intuition has been all that accurate lately, but it's an impression I can't seem to shake.

"Oh, I'm *so* sorry. I didn't see you there."

Jill hardly sounds genuine, and the look I'm getting this time isn't very friendly. Appearing to be on the verge of tears, she turns and disappears back into the crowd.

Now I'm dying to read that note, and I'm starting to wonder how smart it was to invite Marla. What I would give to be alone right now.

Chapter 27

I make my apologies and head for the main bathrooms as soon as we get back to the boat. Debbie offers to give Marla a tour of the boat, and Vinny follows me out of the cabin, heading for one of the deck chairs with the Sunday paper.

"That was a pretty good shot if you ask me," he grins with amusement.

I should have known better than to think he'd missed it.

"Yeah. She has some fight in her, doesn't she?"

"Yes she does. Just be careful, okay?"

"Hey, you know me."

"Yes I do. And that's why I'm saying what I'm saying."

I know he's being sincere and I do appreciate the concern, but I'm not really sure what he's worried about.

"Chenz, she's all I can think about. What else can I say?"

He nods his head.

I turn for the transom door. I need to find some privacy.

Chapter 28

Sitting in the solitude of the last stall, I read it again and again, and I swear that if I were physically capable of doing it, I'd give myself a nice swift kick in the ass.

Dear Michael,
I'm sure you must be furious with me and I can understand why, but PLEASE believe me, I didn't know you had company yesterday and I was wearing that bathing suit only for you. I was tanning on the beach, and I told that lowlife I'm married to I was going to the snack bar, but I was really heading to see you. I know I should have put my shirt on, but I wanted so much for you to notice me the way you did the first time I wore it, so I could tell you I was sorry, and that I loved you, and that I was hoping you'd give me another chance to prove it. When I saw all those people on your boat I didn't know what to do. I was going to turn around right then and there, but I thought it would only make it worse, so I kept on walking by without looking. As soon as I got to my boat I covered myself with another shirt and then I took the shortcut across the sand back to the beach. I swear I did, and I've been a wreck ever since, worrying what you

might be thinking of me. I know I'm wrong about a couple of things, and I'm sorry. PLEASE forgive me, and PLEASE give me another chance. I promise I'll do whatever you want me to.

I love you so much and I need you even more,
Jill

I wish to God I could talk to her right now, apologize for inviting Marla, tell her that I love her too, tell her what an idiot I am for jumping to the wrong conclusions so quickly. I remember thinking it was odd to see her sprinting across the sand so soon after she walked by the boat yesterday. It never occurred to me that such an explanation was possible. And I know deep down inside why that is so. It's because I'm thick in the head and I have a suspicious nature. Once I make up my mind about something, I refuse to consider anything else.

I feel like such a fool, a very heartsick lonely fool, and I have to figure out how to get in touch with her... assuming she'll still speak to me. Unlike her, I have no good excuse for Marla, other than I was being childish and spiteful because I couldn't help myself. I wonder if begging for mercy might work.

Chapter 29

It's been a long, dreadful day - probably the worst I've ever spent at the beach, and I have no one to blame for it but myself. All I can do is thank God the ferry is about to leave and Marla's on it. I can't wait to get rid of her. She's sitting on the upper deck next to the railing, waving goodbye. This has to be the fourth or fifth time she's waved and we still have the better part of five minutes to go. It's becoming a real effort to return the gesture.

Under the best of circumstances she and I would have had our challenges, but given my feelings about Jill, it's impossible to even try. I made a reasonable effort to get along out of respect for Debbie, but there is no way we'll ever be seeing each other again, at least not on purpose. She turned out to be a nice enough person, but we have almost nothing in common, and for some unknown reason I find her generally annoying.

About the only thing that's gone right today is I haven't bumped into Jill again. That would have been extremely awkward after reading her note. Now that Marla's on her way, though, I'm suddenly wondering where she's been hiding and how much damage control might need to be done.

"Isn't she great?" Debbie's waving away all excited.

The Charms Of Fire Island

Vinny's hands are already resting in his pockets, and I decide it's a good time to join him. I'll let Debbie be the official waver for the group. She's very good at it, and I think Vinny and I do a better job of just nodding and smiling, sort of backing her up.

"She sure is." I agree.

I'll break the ugly news to her later. I don't want to spoil the moment.

Chapter 30

Strong wind is gusting out of the east, driving rain so hard against the bridge enclosure it sounds like someone's shooting it with a hose. A bolt of lightning just flashed to the north, and I can already hear the heavy sound of thunder as it begins to rumble across the dark, ominous sky. The forecast I heard only yesterday afternoon called for partly cloudy, but I have to commend Mother Nature for the nasty surprise. It's a much more fitting way to wrap up a disastrous weekend.

The morning air is chilly for the Fourth of July, made even worse by the soaking wet shirt I'm wearing, but I wouldn't have traded having my coffee up here for a faster and dryer climb up the ladder. I raise the thick mug to my lips as I glance around the marina once again, my eyes uncontrollably coming to rest on the same empty slip, the one that Jill was in.

I can't believe they left during the middle of the night, and I can only guess as to the reason why. I haven't seen her since Marla's arrival, and I'm beginning to think I'm in more serious trouble than I had figured. I left her cell phone out on the table last night hoping she might wander by to get it back, but it's still sitting there covered in rain, probably ruined. I had another fitful night of sleep, followed by even more misery than yesterday.

A strike of lightning startles me and I jump sufficiently to spill some of the coffee. Wonderful. I don't see anything handy lying around to wipe up the mess, so I pull off my shirt. It's shot to hell anyway. A deafening clap of thunder finishes the one-two punch, pumping new vigor into the pounding rain. It's not a good time to be refilling my coffee cup, so I rise from the helm chair and move to the forward bench. I can lie out more comfortably there.

I have got to find a way to get control of my emotions, somehow adjust my frame of mind to focus on something other than her. This whole situation is ridiculous, and the more I think about it, the more I'm sure there's no way to rationally justify how strongly I desire her companionship. But that's the problem with emotions, they are what they are, and you can't necessarily make sense of them. When it comes right down to it, I know it's as much about sex as it is anything else, probably even more so. Not that I think there's anything wrong with reaching that conclusion. I've always felt it was the cornerstone for any meaningful relationship. Show me a man who doesn't feel that way. Sure I want a woman to be my partner, someone I respect as my equal, tackling every challenge the world can throw at us together, an inseparable team. I couldn't imagine being truly happy with anything less than that. But I also want the very sight of her to be a constant reminder of how special she makes me feel in bed, and relish in the pleasure and contentment of knowing she feels the same way about me: that I mean everything to her.

I want it to be the way it was at first with Gina.

Look at the year or so I wasted with Allison. Not only did she fail to impress me in general as a desirable partner, she never once totally satisfied me sexually. Then, along comes Jill: smart, charming, beyond beautiful, good sense of humor, and most amazingly, better in the sack than Gina was. Now, that fact alone may suggest I've lived too sheltered a life, that I need to get out more and search a little harder, that there are probably a multitude of woman running around all over the place who can put even Jill to shame when it comes to great sex. But, first of all, I find that impossible to believe, and second of all, I don't really care if there are. I couldn't imagine the time and suffering involved in having to test out the theory, with the odds being far more likely that I'll run into another Allison, or worse.

No.

I believe in fate, and it was fate that brought us together. And when I put things more clearly in perspective, there's really only one problem here - she's married, though not by choice, to a bully capable of murder, and she fears for her life. Well, I've dealt with my share of bullies over the years, and even if he did kill someone in cold blood, he's still no different than the rest, and you need to handle him the same way - you beat the hell out of him and scare *him* half to death, because that's the only language he understands.

It's becoming more and more apparent that Vinny had the best idea, the one that's essentially risk free. It might take more time than I would like, but that's about the only downside. And as much as I hate having someone else do my dirty work, I simply can't afford to get caught doing something stupid myself.

So what I will do is hire some professional street thugs to brutalize Dave on a regular basis. I won't hire them directly, but through an agent that deals in that kind of service. This way, it winds up being a third party doing the damage that no one can ever trace back to me. It'll cost me a total of ten grand a performance to line up some degenerate to stalk him out at his favorite bar, instigate a fight, and break a few of his bones. Then in a month or two when he finally gets the casts off, they'll do it again. And they'll keep doing it until he reaches a point where he has no life left in him to fight anyone ever again, including his wife. He'll probably be so busted up after a year or so, that she'll be able to kick *his* ass.

I'm smiling as I think about it some more, and I know it's a little sick to be finding humor in all this. But it just occurred to me to make sure they break his right leg the first time so he won't be able to drive. That'll give us a lot more freedom to see each other right away, without having to worry about him popping out of the woodwork.

All I have to do now is hope and wait for her to call me so I can apologize, and then I'll tell her the plan.

Chapter 31

Twice I've tried to call her house, using two different pay phones on opposite sides of town. Yesterday I got the answering machine, and today I got Dave. I don't know what else I can do.

I thought of hiring Peter Long to stake out her house and let me know if she goes out somewhere, like to the mall or a supermarket. Then I could rush there to *accidentally* bump into her. But I can't do it. It seems too sleazy and disingenuous. As much as I want her, I don't think I should have to do something like that to make it happen if it's truly meant to be. After all, while I can, to a large extent, understand her being upset with me, it was in fact her fault that Marla came into the picture in the first place. She's the one who dumped me to start with. How was I to know she would change her mind so quickly?

Every time the phone rings, I take a deep breath before I answer it, thinking this time it has to be the one. And each time I hear a voice that isn't hers, I feel sicker than before. Work has never felt so much like work, and all I do in the evening in mope around the house... waiting.

Staring up at a tiny spot the painter missed on the ceiling, I'm thinking that I should be hungry, but I'm not. I reach for the extra pillow, pulling it in close to my chest as I roll to my right, wrapping my legs firmly around the length of it. Maybe hugging something might relieve some of the anguish. How I would love to be holding her now. Tomorrow makes an entire week since we last made love on the beach.

I've become so used to false alarms that it's hard to get excited when I hear the sound of an engine... like the one I could swear is approaching now. I've been fooled at least a dozen times over the past several nights by cars pulling into the house in front of me. But this time it's different, I'm sure of it.

There's a car coming up my driveway! I spring from the bed and step to the window, barely soon enough to see the red glow of a taillight disappearing under the overhang of the garage. I couldn't see the rest of the car, but I just know it's her.

There was no phone call, and I don't hear the garage door opener; both of which probably indicate I'm still in the doghouse, big time. But I don't care about that right now. I know everything will be all right as soon as I get the chance to explain myself and apologize. Oh my god... and then we get to make up. She wouldn't have come here if making up weren't part of the plan. The thought of that is almost too mind-boggling to dwell on, but it nevertheless begins to overwhelm me as I hurry down the stairs.

I'm not going to get too sloppy, but I am going to make sure she knows how sorry I am about the Marla situation, that I never meant to upset her as much as I did, and that she never needs to worry about it happening again. It wasn't intentional, and I'm not one to play games; I just didn't realize how much she really cared for me. But I'm thrilled to death to know that now, and I deserved every bit of the lesson it took for me to find it out the hard way. From now on, we talk things out. No more jumping to conclusions fueled by silly unfounded jealousy.

The bell rings just as I get to the door, my head is spinning with emotion. I pause for a moment to gather myself before I pull it open. Maybe if I sneak a peek through the peephole, I can tell what kind of mood she's in.

"Oh... no. This can't be happening." The words escape from my mouth involuntarily. What could I have possibly done to deserve this?

I can't even describe how lousy I've come to feel in about one nanosecond. If only I hadn't switched on the light, I could have pretended I wasn't home. This is worse than a nightmare. At least I wake up from those. Damn it! I swing it open slowly, dreading the confrontation that awaits me.

"Allison? What are you doing here? Did I forget to send you something?" I ask as nicely as I can manage, backing up just enough to let her gain a small foothold in the foyer.

As soon as she smiles I can tell she's had too much to drink - it's uncharacteristically loose and friendly, the normal stiffness is missing. It looks like she's having trouble standing, and her blouse is unbuttoned so far down her chest, the black lacy cups of her bra are more than half exposed. All things considered, not a pretty picture.

"*Nope*. I think you even sent extra." The words are slurred and the smile's getting sloppier. "That's why I wanted to come by and thank you."

"Well that was very thoughtful of you, but hardly necessary."

"Yes it was!" she announces with a louder voice, her head now bobbing back and forth. "Because I have a little surprise for you."

She's running at full speed ahead, and the reality check I'm about to hit her with won't be well received. But then again, I really have no other options because I'm not about to entertain her. I'd rather choke her to death for getting me so worked up over nothing.

"Look, Allison, I was just getting ready for bed... So if you don't mind..."

"I don't mind at all," she says sweetly, still smiling as her right hand reaches up for my face. "I'm sorry, okay, and I want to come upstairs and show you how sorry I am."

"No." I hold my left hand up to fend her off gently. "It's over Allison."

Her smile loses a little steam, but I can tell she's not going down easy. As if her shirt wasn't already open enough, she loosens another button.

"Don't you want to see what I'm wearing for you?"

"I can already see most of it, and I'm not kidding around Allison. It's over."

Her hand moves down to the waist of my gym shorts, getting in a slight tug before I grab her wrist firmly and pull it away.

"Allison! Knock it off! It's over!" Now I'm pissed.

I see the left hand coming, but I decide to let her have one. Maybe it'll satisfy her enough to make her go away. It was a good shot though, and the side of my face is stinging.

"I hope that made you feel good. But I promise, if you do it again, I'll slap you back so hard that I'll knock you flat on your ass."

Here comes the frown, followed by the crying.

"You bastard! All you ever did was use me!"

This is too much, and what I feel like doing more than anything else is pushing her out the door and slamming it in her face. The problem is, she's too upset and intoxicated to be driving, and I would feel terrible if something bad happened to her.

"I'm sorry Allison, but I'm not going to argue with you. So please let me call you a cab, and I'll drive your car home. The taxi can bring me back."

She appears to be regaining her composure, and I turn to get the phone.

"Screw you Michael!" she yells at my back, halfway across the room.

I guess she figured on me chasing her, because she's already out the door running for her car, but I can't seem to muster up the energy. At least I made the offer. The engine sounds a lot like it did the last time she left in a hurry. I only hope she has enough sense to slow it down once she hits the main drag.

As I stand there listening to the sound of the engine fade, my head suddenly slumps. I'm feeling totally exhausted. I shut the door, turn out the lights, and head back upstairs to my pillows.

Chapter 32

"Six ball down there."

He points to the far corner. Another shot made easy by having good cue ball position. I'm about to lose again.

"Eight ball in the side."

I nod, accepting defeat.

"Nice game Chenz. I think I've had enough."

"Me too. I haven't seen you shoot this lousy in years."

"Oh you're just saying that to make me feel better."

We shake hands smiling, and then he puts his arm around my shoulder, leading us back to our drinks at the bar.

The Clipper is a simple enough place, directly on the water in Babylon. It's about four or five miles west of Bay Shore, and almost directly south of the shop. It offers basic food like chicken wings and burgers, and has a few scattered televisions that are always tuned in to some kind of sporting event. For the more "active clientele" like us, there's a dartboard and a pool table. It tends to draw more of a business crowd during the week, suits and ties stopping for a couple of pops before they head home for dinner. We don't come here too often, but often enough to know a few of the regulars.

Vinny and I got here ahead of the twins and Fat Tony. We left the shop right after lunch to pick up our new cars and then came directly over. It's coming up on five o'clock now though, and I just caught a glimpse of one of the Carbone's passing through the front parking lot.

"So what's your next move?"

"I don't know Chenz. I really don't. I'm starting to wonder whether something bad has happened to her. It doesn't make sense to write a note like she did and then not give me a chance to explain myself."

"Why do you think I keep telling you not to get too attached? Because the closer you get to a woman, the more you want to try to figure her out, and that's impossible. Hell… I'd give you better odds on one of the twins figuring out the Dewey Decimal System."

I smile. "That bad huh?"

"Yeah, I'm afraid so. And that's why you have to stay loose, have fun, and let them try to figure *you* out. Hey, if you're interested, Rebecca says she has a very hot looking friend that would love to meet you."

Rebecca was our car saleswoman, the one I was sure Vinny would have dinner with. He has, twice already.

I'm not really in the mood to debate our differing views again in regard to relationships. In his own way, I know he's being sincere.

"Thanks, but I made that mistake once already. I'm not doing anything stupid this time until I'm sure of the score."

He nods his head. "Okay. I understand."

"Vinny!" They call it out in unison, barely inside the front door.

He raises his left arm to answer the greeting.

"Here comes half the entertainment," he grins, holding his glass up to me.

I tap mine against his, and we both take a drink.

"Hello Michael." Joe says, as he gets closer.

"What do you say Joe. Frank." We all shake hands.

"So what's going down?" Vinny asks, waving the bartender over.

Frank orders a couple of beers and moves in closer so no one else can hear him. It's not too hard to tell he's enjoying himself, his chuckles are sounding more like snorts.

"Everything went according to plan so far. Danny, or Danielle, or whatever his name is, said he had Tony so hot last night he could hardly stand it. He was stroking him under the table at dinner, and teased him all the way to the motel."

"Then he made Tony take his clothes off first," Joe whispers excitedly, straining not to laugh, "figuring he wouldn't chase him if he was naked."

"He asked him if he could keep a secret," Frank's starting to lose it, "which of course Tony was more than happy to promise. So he told him to lie down on the bed and close his eyes."

"And that's when he whipped it out!"

Frank gives Joe an elbow for saying it too loud, but with all of us laughing at the same time, I'm sure everyone else figured it was the tail end of a joke.

"Man! He must have freaked out." Vinny says it almost as if he feels sorry for the guy. Like he momentarily put himself in Fat Tony's shoes. I shake my head to clear that same thought.

"Yeah," Frank confirms it with a big smile of satisfaction. "Tony chased him halfway across the parking lot before he remembered he was naked."

"So where's Danny boy now?" Vinny asks.

"Outside in his car," Joe says. "We told him to wait until Tony gets here, and give us about five minutes before he comes in."

"Speak of the devil."

I nod towards the door - Fat Tony just made his entrance.

Not halfway across the room, he's already bellowing for a Jameson on the rocks and pointing to the spot on the bar where he wants it delivered to. It looks like he'll be sharing the corner with us. This is perfect.

Watching him swagger over, I'm finding it easy to enjoy the moment. If I went through what he did last night, I'd be hiding somewhere, keeping a very low profile. But he appears as arrogant and full of himself as ever.

"*Vinny... Michael*," he graces us with the first hello, "how are my parts coming?"

"Parts are fine Tony," I'm glad he asked. "Just make sure you have the cash ready."

I can tell he's sorry that he brought it up. I nod my head to emphasize how serious I am, and he finally nods back. Then he focuses on the twins.

"You two still owe me an answer on that chip credit I want. I hope you haven't forgotten about that. Tuesday's the deadline."

"Not a chance Tony," Frank assures him. "In fact, you're going to have it before then."

"Well that's *good!*" he barks with a serious looking nod, no doubt expecting nothing less than full compliance with his demands.

"Hey! You guys should have seen Tony in action last Friday night," Joe starts it off, "he had this hot young thing all over him."

"Is that right?" Vinny plays along.

"Yeah, he was really pouring on the old charm."

"Forget about last Friday!" he's already pissed.

"Come on Tony, you had that babe on fire."

"I said forget it!"

"Why, that's her right there!" Frank points as "she" walks in the door, heading right for us. "What do you think about that Vinny?"

"Wow! Not too bad Tony. I guess you still got the touch."

Tony's not looking, but I can see his face is turning red.

"Buy a lady a drink?" Danielle's standing right next to him.

"Get the hell away from me or I'll kill you!" His head doesn't move.

"Hey! *Tony*," Vinny chides him, "is that any way to speak to a lady?"

"She's nah…" he catches himself before he finishes, then turns to face "her". "You have *some fucking nerve* coming back in here. What do you want?"

"Don't worry Tony, this is the last you'll ever see of me. I just needed to give you a message."

Danielle strikes a pose and points a feminine looking finger at the twins.

"It's from those two."

Tony looks at the twins, puzzled.

"What?"

Neither of them can keep a straight face, and I think Tony's starting to realize he's been had. He turns back to Danielle.

"What are you talking about?"

"They wanted me to give you the answer on the chip credit question," he says sweetly.

"The *chip credit* question?"

"Yeah… They said it's hanging right here between my legs," he reaches down to grab it for effect, "you know, the thing I showed you last night."

"You little faggot!"

Tony roars as he grabs for him, but Danielle's too fast. He ducks once, and he's already halfway out the door.

The four of us are howling, and I've never seen Tony so furious as he turns on the twins.

"So you two little dickheads think you're pretty fucking funny huh? Well let me tell you something. Keep right on laughing, because you will *never* do work for me again. Ever!

"Well let me tell *you* something Tony," Joe stands into him, probably hoping Tony takes the first swing - "We have a whole bunch of finished parts you need real bad, and you're not getting a single one of them until you pay for them all. What do you think about that?"

Suddenly, Tony doesn't look so good.

"Don't be ridiculous! I don't have that kind of cash sitting around collecting dust."

Frank gets right in his face. "Then you better find it somewhere fast... Asshole!"

Chapter 33

I hear the sound, but it feels like something I can't get to. It must be the third or fourth ring that finally does the trick, and then I blink my eyes a few times, trying to help my fumbling fingers locate the phone.

"Hello." I barely get it out of my mouth.

Nothing.

Now I'm coming around quickly.

"Hello?"

I hear soft crying. My heart begins to race as I sit up in bed.

"Jill? Is that you?"

There's more soft sobbing.

"Is that Marla person still with you?" she's choking on the words.

"Oh Jill. She was never *with* me. Are you okay? I've been so worried about you."

"Michael, please, don't lie to me. I need to know the truth."

"I'm not lying, I swear to you. She was nothing more than a friend of a friend. And yes, I was an idiot for inviting her over… but it meant absolutely nothing to me, you have to believe me. I got rid of her that same afternoon, and I've been sick ever since I read your note. I've been praying for the chance to apologize for being so childish."

The Charms Of Fire Island

I think that came out a bit more pathetic than I would have liked, but I don't care. That's how I feel. I want her to know how desperate I am to be with her again. How much I love and miss her.

"Jill, I'm telling you the God's honest truth. I swear it."

She starts crying a little harder and I'm hoping that's good.

"I've been afraid to call. I thought I lost you."

It feels great to hear her say that the way she did.

"You thought *you* lost *me?* Let me tell you something, I've been a basket case worrying that you wouldn't forgive me, that I'd never see you again."

"Well that makes two of us... I kept trying to convince myself that I'd be okay without you, but it hasn't worked out very well. I miss you so much, and I can't stand not knowing where you are and who you might be with... that someone else might be taking my place."

"Hey, unless you decide to dump me again," my voice becomes playful, "I'm not planning on going anywhere. That much I promise. From now on I'm sticking to you like glue."

She laughs softly with a sigh of relief, "That sounds messy."

"Sometimes messy is good."

"Oh yeah? Like when you make love to me?"

"Hey, was that a shot?"

"Not even close. I love the messes you make," her tone is now teasing, "especially when you make them in my mouth."

I am so horny I can't stand it.

"Are you trying to drive me completely out of my mind? Because if you are, you're doing a damn good job of it."

Her laughter is once again ever so soft.

"And you think the sound of your voice alone doesn't make me wet between my legs? Right where I love to feel the magic of your tongue?"

Amazing. I've wondered at times how a company selling phone sex could ever make a buck, but I'm rapidly getting a better appreciation for the possibilities. It suddenly occurs to me she must have a decent amount of privacy to be talking like this. Looking at the clock I see it's four thirty in the morning.

"Where are you?"

"I'm just sitting in my car… in your driveway."

"What?" I scramble out of bed. "Why didn't you tell me? How come you didn't come to the door?"

"I thought she might be with you, and I couldn't have handled that. I was too scared to ring the bell without calling first. Is it okay if I come in?"

"Is it *okay?* I'll be down in about one second. Give me two if I manage to trip and fall down the stairs."

Chapter 34

She looks like an angel lying there asleep on her side, such a beautiful face. The curves of her body so well toned and perfectly shaped, her long soft hair flowing up from the bed behind her. It's covering almost half of her breast, just shy of the nipple, which is relaxed now but hardly flattened. They seem to have a natural firmness all their own.

I hate having to wake her up, but breakfast is almost ready, and she did insist on no more than an hour of sleep. Plus, if I stand here much longer thinking about how much I still crave her touch, I'll be all worked up again in no time. I can feel the little guy starting to stir already. We have all day, and I need to pace myself.

"Hey." I call to her softly, placing my hand on her shoulder as I sit on the bed. "Jill? Breakfast is almost ready sweetheart."

She moans very little protest as she opens her eyes, bringing her right hand up to the side of my neck. "Oh... Michael," she says it slow and soft, "it feels so good to wake up to you."

I caress her shoulder as I move my hand across it, and then on to the side of her face.

"You hungry?"

"Very... and it smells wonderful."

She rolls away from me slightly, onto her back, getting in a quick yawn as she stretches her arms up and over her head. Then with her arms still extended, she angles back to me, reaching up, a warm smile on her face.

"But couldn't we play in bed for a few minutes first?"

My concern about stamina comes to mind, and after giving it some careful consideration, there's no doubt what I must do.

I move towards her, slowly stroking the inner sides of her thighs, and then massaging the flat of her stomach, making my way steadily up to her breasts. Her hands come to rest against the sides of my head, pulling me gently down to her.

I'll start pacing myself right after this.

Chapter 35

"This is such a terrific place," she moves into my arms as she says it, joining her hands behind my back, "and what an amazing sunset. Thanks for sharing it with me."

"I'm glad you liked it. It is beautiful, isn't it?"

"It's beyond beautiful. It's enchanting. I'm just sorry we can't stay for the night."

"Soon we will. I promise."

"I can't wait."

We're anchored off of Fire Island at a place called Sailors Haven, about four miles east of Atlantique. The marina itself is very small and far from anything fancy, but it's also home to the Sunken Forest, which is an extraordinary national wilderness preserve. It has something like forty acres of unspoiled hardwood groves, marshes, and sand dunes, with the secondary dunes near the ocean being so high; it makes the forest appear to be sunken. In reality it's just an illusion; the ground here is no deeper than the rest of the island.

We ran the dinghy up on the beach earlier this afternoon and ventured the maze of narrow quiet boardwalks. She couldn't get enough of it, unable to believe some of the trees were two to three hundred years old. We walked all the way through it at least once, talking and laughing about one thing or another, never having trouble finding a vacant bench when we felt like resting. I don't think anyone else I've ever brought here has enjoyed it so much, and I'm really glad I thought of coming.

Back on the boat a few hours later, we drank a small pitcher of margaritas sitting in the shade of the cockpit. No more than a handful of boats could have passed by the entire time. She had never played *Pass The Pigs* before, and we got more than a few laughs out of those little porkers - rolling two tiny rubber pigs the same as you would dice, and either getting points or losing points based on the way they land. It involves more luck than anything else, but just watching the pigs land in all sorts of funny looking positions is pretty entertaining.

For dinner I grilled some salmon steaks on the barbecue, and she insisted on making the risotto. It felt really good having a woman help me put a meal together for a change. It's been a long time.

"We could do it again tomorrow if you'd like, or we could head further east to Watch Hill. They have a nice secluded nature trail there as well."

"Either one sounds great to me, but don't forget I have to be home by early afternoon. Don't you think we might be better off staying closer to home?"

How quickly such unpleasant things slip my mind. "Yeah, I suppose you're right. I'll think of something else."

Dave left at three this morning for Montauk Point to do some deep-sea fishing with the boys. It's an overnight charter, so he won't be back until sometime after lunch tomorrow. Her curfew tonight is ten-thirty, and he'll be calling home as usual to check on her. How pathetic, I can't wait to take this guy out.

I told her my plan earlier, and it made her kind of nervous at first. She was understandably concerned about living with him once he's been battered, how he might become vengeful, and take things out on her. She was also worried about him not being able to go to work. It seems that the unpaid bills have been piling up at a faster rate lately. I'm sure the fishing trip to Montauk hasn't helped things either. But ultimately she agreed, keeping her promise to follow my lead, and that in itself is all I could ask for. Thinking about it some more though, I'm wondering what's to be gained by her staying with him anyway? Why drag the whole thing out so much? She was always afraid to leave him because she feared him coming after her, but I now have the means to make sure that doesn't happen. I don't care what it costs me.

"Now here's an idea. Why not pull up the stakes and move out, right after he's beaten up the first time?"

"What?"

"I'm just thinking. Why don't you leave the son of a bitch as soon as he takes the first beating? Come and live with me right away. Believe me, he won't be in any condition to come looking for you once he's had his little altercation. I'll make absolutely certain of it."

"Gee... I don't know. Won't that appear sort of obvious?"

"So what if it does? Amuse me for a minute, and let me know where I stop making sense... From what you tell me, it's common knowledge you two fight on a regular basis, and that he drinks to excess just about every day of his life. On top of that, you've come to find out he's made a complete mess of your financial situation, and you're close to being in the poor house. And then, to top it all off, he gets himself busted up so badly while he's out getting drunk running his mouth, that he can't even go to work. If you ask me, it sounds like enough to send any woman packing."

She says nothing for a few seconds. "Well, I guess when you say it like that, it doesn't sound so bad. But won't my living with you right off the bat screw up any divorce settlement I might have been entitled to?"

"Probably. But it doesn't sound like there's very much there to be worried about in the first place. And besides, I have more than enough money to take care of you, much better than he ever did. Trust me on that."

The side of her head comes to rest against my chest as she squeezes into me. I say nothing more as I hold her fast, letting her have some time to think about it.

"It's hard to believe this is happening so quickly. But everything you're saying seems to make a lot of sense, and God knows I've been praying for something like this to happen for a long time... How soon are we talking about?"

"Well, from what I'm told, if I'm able to make initial contact on Monday or Tuesday, it should only take about a week after that."

I feel her head nodding. "Okay then, count me in," she says firmly, as she looks up into my eyes, "I'm all yours."

The kiss is soft and long, but less urgent than earlier, like there's a sudden understanding between us that we have less need to rush. We'll soon have all the time we want together.

We finally release each other, and I turn to grab what's left of our wine. I'm sure it's time we finished up and headed home.

"I know this isn't going to make you happy," she breaks the mood, "but we're supposed to be going up to his uncle's cabin this coming weekend."

She's right. I don't like the thought of that at all.

"I'm sorry, but I had already started the wheels in motion before you convinced me not to run him over with the boat. And not knowing where I stood with you, the idea of going up there seemed much more appealing than coming to Atlantique and seeing you there with another woman. Then Karen and Joe... they're one of the couples that come to Atlantique a lot… asked if they could come up on Saturday and spend the night."

"When were you and Dave planning to go?"

"Friday morning."

I feel myself frown.

"Look, Michael, in the grand scheme of things it's really not that important, and I'll fake being sick again like I did last week at Atlantique if you want me to. But Karen is about the only one of the group I feel somewhat close to, and it would sort of give me the opportunity to make sure she knows how unhappy I've become with Dave. You know, maybe grease the skids a little."

In reality, whether she goes up there or she stays down here, she'll be with him most of the time anyway. At least up there, she'll have a friend along some of the time. I'm so close to having her all to myself, I can taste it. But now more than ever, I've got to be patient.

"No. It's okay. You should probably go and spend the time with Karen like you said. What matters most to me is that you told me about it now, and that you would have backed out if I had asked you to. Just be careful, okay?"

"Don't worry, I will. And thanks for understanding."

Chapter 36

We stayed fairly close to home this morning as Jill suggested, figuring it made no sense to push the envelope. There's a string of smaller islands on this end of the bay that she's passed numerous times heading to and from Atlantique, and she jumped at the chance to explore them a little closer in the Whaler. I like doing it by myself now and then, when I'm in the mood to kill some time in solitude, but I haven't done it with another woman since before Gina and I were married. We used to spend hours idling around those mostly isolated shorelines, finding just the right spot to get naked and intimate on a summer afternoon.

It took a good part of the morning to show her everything I thought worth seeing, and we finally found a spot we liked on one of the tinier, unnamed islands - a small white strip of sand with scattered trees and bushes, not quite enough for complete privacy, but with nobody else in sight it was enough to make us want to take the chance. It was the first time Jill ever made love among the throes of nature in broad daylight, and it had the effect of heightening her wildness to the point where it became contagious. Our climax was so powerful, it literally shook us to the core, frantically clinging to each other as if our very lives depended on it.

Once the incredible excitement was behind us, though, we didn't linger very long, thinking it might be smarter to resume a more innocent looking boat ride. But what a memory it made for, certainly not something I'll forget anytime soon.

Standing beside me now as we idle back into the marina, her hand closes tightly on the one I have resting on the center console. Out of sight from wandering eyes along the pier, our fingers begin to gently struggle with the pending farewell. We agreed earlier to part without hugging or kissing, there's nothing to be gained from demonstrating too much affection on a public dock. I keep telling myself we have only one lousy week to go, but right now that week is starting to feel like an eternity.

We once again left her car in the parking lot at the end of the canal, and from what I can see, all looks well as we approach the pilings. There's a few people sitting in lounge chairs tending crab traps, and there's an old lady holding a fishing pole fastened to a red and white plastic bobber, but that's about it. I have to make sure I keep it calm and cool now, because all she needs is for me to falter on this goodbye, and I'm sure she's going to lose it too. Wouldn't that create a spicy sight for these otherwise casual spectators.

Accepting my hand, she steps to the gunwale and onto the dock. Turning back to face me, she scrunches her nose, trying her best to make a funny face but appearing more like she's ready to cry.

"I love you," she says it only loud enough for me to hear.

"I love you too. Don't forget that."

She nods, turning away quietly, slowly walking the few yards over to her car. I wait until she's got it started and ready to go, and then as she heads for the exit we both wave our final goodbye. I see her hand brushing the sides of her cheeks before she lowers it.

That was pretty upsetting, but I have to keep myself focused on the bigger picture.

Chapter 37

Nearing the dock at my house, I'm surprised to see Vinny with the Tiki bar open for business. The last he told me, he was spending all day at the beach. Someone had organized a big volleyball game down by the ocean, and he was planning on playing.

One thing that doesn't surprise me is that the business appears to be entirely female: three of them, all in bikinis. Even from here I can see him smiling as he talks to them. He's got on one of his Hawaiian party shirts, and he's wearing the big straw hat that he keeps in the cabana for such special occasions. The girls are all leaning in closely from the opposite side of the bar, no doubt being entertained by one of his more amusing stories. As soon as I switch off the outboard engine, I hear the slowing whine of the blender, gradually giving way to the stereo. He's got on some soft tropical background music to complete the ambiance.

"Michael!" He lifts the pitcher from the base, holding it up in my direction. "You're just in time! Hey! Any idea what we did with those little drink umbrellas?"

They all turn at the same time to check me out, and judging by looks alone, I think he must have struck the mother load: two blondes and a brunette, three pairs of long slender legs, and everyone of them gorgeous. I wouldn't be surprised if they were all models.

"They're in the bottom drawer on the right!" I call out as I finish tying the line.

"So what happened to the day at the beach? The volleyball game?" I ask, walking over.

"First of all," he declares firmly as he starts to pour the drinks, "you must let me introduce you to these beautiful guests of ours. Ladies, this is Michael, our host. And Michael, this is April, Summer, and Sherry." He uses his free hand to point them out as he goes.

"It's nice to meet you Michael. This is quite a place you have," Summer says, taking the lead, and the other two smile along.

"Thank you. I'm glad you like it."

"Join us?" Vinny's still holding up the pitcher, getting every mile he can out of being the exotic bartender, but he knows very well I don't drink rum.

"No. Thanks Chenz. But I'll take a beer if you don't mind."

"Coming right up!"

"So what happened to the volleyball game?"

"You're looking at it," he spreads his arms as he says it, "that's how we met."

"And it was a lucky thing for us too," April turns to tell me, "Vinny rescued us today."

"Yeah," Sherry confirms it, "this big muscle-bound creep kept bothering us, and after Vinny told him to stop it a few times, he finally knocked him flat on his ass."

"Right there in front of everyone," Summer adds, "it was so cool."

Now he's smiling hard enough that it's starting to look goofy.

I shake my head as if I'm not buying it.

"And I'm supposed to believe you gave some guy several chances before you finally decked him?"

"He sure did," Sherry says. "He was being very polite, right up until the big jerk pushed him, and that's when he had enough. He punched that guy out in about two seconds flat."

Looking at him, I can't help smiling.

"You know Chenz, I think you're starting to mellow out on me."

I'm sure that in reality, he was playing it up for all it was worth, taking his time and savoring the opportunity to impress these lovely girls.

"Hey Michael, it's Sunday!" His hands are up in the air again with the palms open. "You know how much I hate violence on Sundays."

"Oh yeah. Sorry. I almost forgot." I laugh as I raise my glass. "Here's to the most peaceful and sensitive guy I know… at least on Sundays."

We all drink. The girls are laughing now too.

"So was this your first visit to Atlantique?" I ask. "I don't remember seeing any of you there before."

"Yeah, we usually go down to Ocean Beach or Ocean Bay Park," April says, "but Bootleggers... that's where we work... was promoting this volleyball game, and so we all came over to play."

Now this is starting to make some sense. Girls this pretty, looking for action, don't normally flock to Atlantique. Not unless they have a nice boat to hang out on, and desirable men to go with it. I've heard of Bootleggers before; it's a classy strip joint up on the north shore.

"Vinny's coming up to see us dance on Thursday," Sherry announces. "Why don't you come along with him? We'll make sure you have a real good time."

"Thanks, that sounds like a lot of fun. Maybe I will."

There's not a chance in hell I'm going anywhere near the place, but agreeing is a lot easier than telling the truth.

Chapter 38

"Okay my friend, everything's set to go. Unless something unforeseen happens, the first attitude adjustment seminar is scheduled for next Tuesday, a week from today."

As much as it bothers me, Vinny insisted he had to be the one to set this thing up. He claims the people he's dealing with don't want to know who's really paying for the service, and I suppose that argument has some merit. However, my better sense tells me he's just trying to protect me. Not that I don't have tremendous appreciation for the way he feels, and God knows I'd do the same for him, but I would never forgive myself if he were to somehow wind up in serious trouble because he did this for me.

Standing there in front of me, he's like a pillar of confidence. I can't help but think how fortunate I am to have such a trusting and loving friend. Already up from my chair, I come around the desk to give him a hug. "Thanks Chenz... I don't know what else to say."

It's a short solid hug, followed by the open palm of his hand lightly tapping my cheek.

"Anytime. You know that."

"I know... Hey, what are you doing for dinner?"

"Sorry. I have plans. I'm looking for something wonderful to happen with Rebecca tonight."

"Oh, very nice. Just try not to forget about our racquetball date tomorrow night."

"Not a chance."

Chapter 39

"Yes!" I holler it out, watching my low shot take a second bounce before Vinny can get to it. "This is it folks!" I'm doing my impersonation of an announcer; *"The Kid* has *The Champ* against the ropes. Who'd a thunk it possible? Already a decisive winner in game one, it looks like *The Kid* might pull off the sweep."

"All right *Kid*, go ahead and serve the ball already, will you?" Vinny's unusually frustrated.

"The crowd settles down now!" I whisper loudly, unable to help it, trying to create an appropriate amount of suspense for such a defining moment in sports history. There's not a soul anywhere in sight, but it pumps me up to make believe there is.

He's not himself tonight, that's for sure, but this is nevertheless sweet redemption for me. I'm able to beat him in racquetball about as often as he beats me in pool, and I've never won two games in a row. We're both dripping wet with sweat, and I'm enjoying every second of it.

Okay Michael, *this is it,* I tell myself. I bounce the ball a couple of times to get my rhythm, and then I go for a low hard drive, deep into the corner behind me. Not only do I get a bit lucky with the placement of the shot, but Vinny wasn't expecting me to go in that direction, and he fails to get there in time.

"It's an ace!" I shout it out. "*The Kid* has taken it to *The Champ!* And the crowd goes wild!"

Tickled to death, I bow to the empty gallery, extending my arms to the invisible masses. Then I turn to shake hands.

"What a game, huh?"

"Did anyone ever tell you what a lousy winner you are?"

He grins slightly, probably more amused than annoyed. But he does have a point.

"Sorry Chenz," I put my arm around his shoulder, "I guess I got a little carried away there."

We start walking to the exit.

"A *little?* Remind me to do hand springs around the bar the next time I beat you in pool."

"Okay, a lot... But do you know how long it's been since I beat you in racquetball?"

"No. How long?"

"It's been so long I can't even remember... Hey, what's the matter with you anyway? You haven't been yourself all day."

We take a seat on the bench just outside the court to cool down a little, both of us resting our forearms against our knees.

"Ahhhhh... you just wouldn't believe what a scene I had at my house last night... I was rolling around the sack with Rebecca, slowly working our way into round two, and all of a sudden, guess who shows up at my door, completely unexpected?"

"That would have to be Debbie."

"Bingo! And believe me when I tell you she went crazy on me, you would have thought we were married. As if I hadn't told her at least a thousand times that I'm not about to get serious with her, or anyone else. Live and let live, you know me, that's my motto."

"So what happened?"

"Ah, she was crying and carrying on about how much she loved me, and that she thought I loved her too. Where does something like that even come from? But on and on she went, and it finally got so bad, I had to go into the bedroom and ask Rebecca to leave. Now try to picture that ugly scene if you can," his head shakes with a look of disgust, "halfway through our first taste of intimacy, and it's shattered by the intrusion of another lover. And then Rebecca has to walk right past her on the way out, with barely enough time to get her clothes on straight."

I can't help but smile at the thought of this drama unfolding in the middle of his living room, with him trying to referee as much peace as possible, probably wearing nothing more than a pair of jockey shorts.

His head continues to shake, but his look becomes more thoughtful. "Let me tell you something, I've got some serious fence mending ahead of me *there* my friend... And then I was up half the night with Debbie, at first trying to console her, reminding her that I've been straightforward since day one, never expecting anything more or less out of her. But around and around we went, not going anywhere fast, and it got to the point where all I wanted to do was just get rid of her and go to sleep. I couldn't take it anymore. You know what I mean?"

"Yeah... I think I do. And some people think that being *you* is easy. If they only knew the half of it... C'mon, lets hit the showers and then I'll buy you a beer."

Chapter 40

I'm relishing the sound of every word, knowing I won't hear her voice again until probably Monday morning. Even if I had gotten the new cell phone in time to give it to her last Sunday, it was doubtful she'd have enough privacy up there to use it anyway. All things considered, though, we've managed pretty well this week, getting in at least one decent conversation every day. I gave her the company PIN number so she could charge the calls, and that's made it much easier.

She's calling me from a pay phone now, up at the mall by her house. They're leaving first thing in the morning, and she snuck out for a few minutes, telling Dave she needed some personal things from the drug store.

"Do you miss me?" she asks.

"Of course I miss you. I can't wait to see you again."

"Do you mean, *see me* the way that only *you* see me?"

"Exactly that way."

"Well that's good to hear... I wasn't going to tell you this, but I bought something extra special from the lingerie shop this afternoon."

Like I'm supposed to believe she just let the cat out of the bag by mistake. To the contrary, she now has me thinking it was the main reason for this parting phone call, to let me know she has something new and sexy, to tantalize me, to make sure I stay focused on her while she's away. We're talking about serious foreplay here, thrilling foreplay as far as I'm concerned, days before we'll have sex again. I love this sort of stuff.

"Oh really? Well that's some exciting news. You have to tell me every last detail."

"Uh uh. That would only spoil the surprise. But I will tell you this… it's very, very naughty looking. It made me wet when I tried it on, thinking about how hard I'm going to make you come the next time I see you."

Now she's killing me. "*You* are such a tease, and you know it. What are you trying to do, send me right over the edge?"

"Yes I am," she laughs softly, "and hopefully it's working. I don't want you to forget me while I'm gone."

"Believe me, there's not even the teeniest, tiniest chance of that happening."

"Well I wanted to make sure, and give you something really nice to look forward to when I get back… I love you."

"I love you too. So be careful."

"Don't worry, I will... And I'll call you as soon as I can... But I have to go now. Okay?"

"Okay sweetheart, I'll see you soon. Bye for now."

"Bye."

I hang up the phone, slipping deep into thought as I stand there slowly shaking my head, trying like hell to think about something other than what she might be wearing the next time I see her. She's incredible, that's for sure, but right now I wish I could get my mind to focus on less exciting thoughts. It's getting painfully crowded just south of my waist.

Maybe I'll pour myself a nice cognac, and try to calm the little guy down some before bedtime.

Chapter 41

"All right, all right, I'm coming!" I yell as loudly as I can, quickly pulling on a pair of shorts. It's not quite eleven thirty, but I was sound asleep. The cognac seems to have hit the intended spot; too bad I couldn't have taken full advantage of it.

Son of a bitch, there it goes again. It sounds like a woodpecker's playing with my doorbell.

"I said alright already! Give me a chance!"

I swear to God, if this is Allison, I'm calling a lawyer tomorrow and getting an order of protection, *for her*, because *she's* going to need it.

Bounding down the stairs still half asleep, I use the handrail more than usual to minimize the odds of breaking my neck. I'm done messing around with the peephole, I can't take the ringing anymore. If this is anything less than a dire emergency, someone's about to get their head chewed off. I'm fully prepared to attack as I open the door, but the person that awaits me is so unexpected the sight of her defuses my temper immediately. It's April, the lone brunette. Her face is covered with tears.

"I'm sorry Michael, but I wasn't sure what to do!" she's hysterical.

Looking behind her I see Vinny's car, and all of a sudden I feel my stomach crowding my throat.

"Where's Vinny?"

She points at the car, and I start running for it.

"What happened?" I'm yelling on the fly.

"Those bastards! They beat him up!" She's gulping for air, staying right on my heels. "I think they put something in his drink. Oh my god, I'm so sorry. I didn't know. I swear I didn't. I would never be part of something like that."

Pulling open the door, there he is, out like a light on the passenger's seat. His face is bruised up pretty bad, and what's left of his shirt reveals a number of nasty cuts and scrapes that are smeared with blood; but his chest is rising and falling steadily and I don't see anything overall that appears too serious. In all the years I've known him, I've never seen my dear friend look even close to this bad, and for an instant I'm overwhelmed with an emotional rush of both anger and sadness. I momentarily dwell too long on the sadness, and I feel the moisture building in my eyes, so I force myself to shake it off and concentrate on what I need to do to help him.

"They threw him into the parking lot like that, and just left him there, laughing."

She's getting worse as she goes.

"I got the girls to help me get him into the car and I came right here. Should I have gone to the hospital?"

"No. No. You did just fine."

"This is terrible. I feel so bad."

I have to get him into the house. I can't leave him out here like this while I'm figuring out what to do.

"*April, stop it now*, it's okay. You did just fine. But you have to help me get him into the house. Can you do that?"

She shakes her head up and down.

"Good girl."

I pull him slowly up and away from the car, taking most of his weight against me. She helps me steady him, through the front door and into the spare bedroom. I saw Dr. Kelly down here earlier on his boat, so he should be home. If not, he's probably at the hospital with another emergency. And if we must go there, we will, but Vinny won't respond well to waking up in one of those places. He hates them with a passion. And regardless of the circumstances, he's got a hell of a lot of pride, and the last thing he'll want to do is deal with a bunch of people standing around feeling sorry for him - or worse, asking him how big and bad the guy was that managed to kick his ass.

I hear it ring for the third time. Come on!

"Hello."

What a relief to hear that voice, but it's not too hard to tell he was sleeping as soundly as I was earlier.

"John. It's Michael."

"Michael? What's going on?"

"Hey, I know it's late, and I'm really sorry, but something's happened to Vinny."

"What? Where are you?"

"At my house. He's been beaten up, maybe drugged. Right now he's unconscious."

"I'll be right there."

"Thanks John."

Chapter 42

Dr. John Kelly has been a friend of ours for several years. We first met him at a local charity golf outing; Vinny and I got teamed up with him and a friend of his to make a foursome. We wound up having so much fun, we started playing together on a regular basis after that. The following year he was having trouble finding a boat slip, and he's been keeping it at my house ever since.

He's in the bedroom with Vinny now, and I'm sitting at the kitchen table with April. She's finally calmed herself down.

"Should we call the police?"

"No. That's not likely an option. Not unless Vinny's in worse shape than I think he is. But I need you to tell me everything you know about what happened."

"There's not a lot to tell," she keeps shaking her head. "We were shown a picture of the two of you, and sent to the beach to get you to come to the club. He told us you two were old friends, and that he was throwing you a surprise party. He was hoping you'd both show up."

"Who is *he?*"

"One of the owners, a guy named Sanchez."

"Ruben Sanchez?" I feel my blood pressure rising.

"Yeah, that's him. Ruben Sanchez, a real creep. But why would he do something like this to such a nice guy?"

"Because he's a dirt-bag."

I should have known that once he surfaced again, he wouldn't go away easy. We, of course, didn't help matters much by sending him that message and stirring up the past. This is the kind of thing I was afraid he was still capable of.

It also doesn't escape my conscience that I'm pretty much the one responsible for all this, and I can't help but wonder how far we'll wind up going with it, and how nasty it will get. Maybe calling the police wasn't such a bad idea, but I couldn't do something like that without first discussing it with Vinny.

I stand as I see John coming out of the bedroom.

"Well, from what I can tell, I suspect you're right about him being drugged, but I'll know for sure once I have this tested."

He holds up a vial of blood.

"How bad is he?"

"If I had my way, he'd be spending the rest of the night in the hospital for observation, but I know how he feels about that, and I doubt it's really necessary. I think he needs sleep more than anything else right now, and he's probably just as well off being here. But keep an eye on him, and call me if you need to.

Otherwise, I'll stop back in the morning on my way to work."

"Hey John, I don't know how to thank you." I hold out my hand.

"That's good to hear," he smiles, "usually I'm the one that feels that way."

It's a nice firm handshake. What a blessing to have a friend like this.

Chapter 43

"I wish I could say, *if you think this looks bad, you should have seen the other guy*, but I didn't see him myself."

I heard the bathroom sink running a few minutes ago. Now he's standing in the kitchen doorway, appearing a bit unsteady, but better than I expected. It's almost five o'clock in the evening, and I'm checking the rib roast I started twenty minutes ago, making sure it's seared enough. Closing the oven door, I turn the temperature down and walk towards him. I was hoping the smell might wake him up.

"That's because you were drugged. You've been sleeping all day."

"Drugged? Oh yeah, the last thing I remember I was ordering a drink at Bootleggers."

He points at his face, "Who did this to me?"

"I hate to have to tell you this, but those three gorgeous looking ladies didn't happen by chance. They were sent to the beach to set us up."

He grimaces, "Now that hurts."

"Well at least they had no idea what was going on. In fact it was April who brought you here last night in a panic. She's still here. She refuses to leave until she knows you're all right and gets to apologize."

He slowly moves his head back and forth, stretching his neck. I'm sure after hearing that, any emotional scars he might have suffered from being setup are already on the mend. I think he's coming around quickly.

"Smells good... Where is she?"

"Thanks. She's outside on the deck, asleep on the chaise lounge. She was up all night with you."

"So who sent them to get us?"

"Ruben Sanchez."

"Ruben... Sanchez."

He repeats it slowly, taking a deep breath and then exhaling in the same tempo, absorbing the news, and undoubtedly contemplating an appropriate reaction.

"It never ceases to amaze me how some people are such gluttons for punishment... I think you and I have a date at Bootleggers in the very near future."

"I already cleared my calendar and put a fresh coat of polish on the old shit kickers. But just remember what you told me about having a lot to lose. Let's make sure we do this right."

"Oh, we'll do it right my friend. That much you can count on."

He glances towards the deck, "Excuse me for a moment, will you?"

"Of course. It's good to see you're feeling better."

He smiles ever so slightly as he turns to go find April.

I head back to the stove and check the potatoes I have boiling in their jackets. A quick stab with the fork tells me they're ready to go. I drain the hot water and replace it with cold, reducing the heat quickly so I can peel them more easily. Then I shred them into a mixing bowl, add some milk, butter, and grated cheese, stir it all together, and scoop it into a casserole dish. I'll throw them in the oven in about ten minutes to finish them off.

I grab the frozen spinach from the freezer, ready to tear the first box open, when the phone rings. Taking advantage of the interruption, I stop for a sip of wine before I answer it, picking it up on the third ring.

I hear the sobbing before it ever reaches my ear, and I know right away this call is about to completely ruin my day.

"Jill? What happened?"

"He... called me... a whore," she's stuttering the words, trembling, "and then... he... beat me."

Oh my god... That son of a bitch! I'm going to beat him beyond senseless.

"Where are you? How bad are you hurt?" I keep my voice as calm as I can.

"I'm in the car. I took off... when... when he went to the bathroom. I'm a few miles down the road, outside of a diner near the thruway."

Thank God for that. "Are you bleeding?"

"Only my nose, a little."

"It's okay now, you hear me? Try to calm down. Everything's going to be okay."

"No! *Michael*, it's not. He's really flipped out this time... He got the cell phone bill this week, and he saw your number on it from the night I was in your driveway. But being the animal that he is he didn't tell me right away. He's been drinking all day, asking me all kinds of questions about where I go, and who I see. I kept telling him he was crazy. But then he shoved the phone bill in my face, and he just started hitting me." Her sobbing gets heavier now. "Is Vinny okay?"

"Stop crying so hard, he's doing fine. Wait a minute, how do you know about Vinny?"

"Because he said that him and some of his partners beat Vinny up last night. He was laughing like a lunatic when he said it."

The thought of this cowardly scumbag punching and kicking my unconscious friend makes me feel like putting my fist through the wall. But instead I bring my clenched hand up against my cheek, holding it firmly there while I listen, trying my best to keep my breathing steady.

"And then he said they're coming after you next. And then, he said..." The last words got caught in her throat. "He told me... Joe and Karen aren't coming up here tomorrow, because some guy named Ruben is coming with a couple of friends..."

Now her sobbing is really out of control.

"He said... he said I have to help him pay off some of our debts, and he wants me to screw all these guys while he watches, so he can see how much of a whore I really am... *I'm telling you, he's out of his mind!*"

I close my eyes, trying to remain calm and collect my thoughts. She's right - he's totally lost it. This is what I was afraid of. I've seen it happen before. People snap from being overwhelmed with torment and stress, they wind up going from one extreme to the other, completely irrational and very dangerous; sort of the way I'm feeling right now myself.

I glance quickly towards the door leading to the deck to make sure I'm still alone.

"Jill. Listen. I'm coming to get you, okay? Is it safe for you to wait where you are?"

"I... I think so. The parking lot is sort of big and open, I can see everyone coming and going. Would you do that? Would you come for me?"

It's now a much softer cry, a cry of relief.

"Oh Michael, thank you. I'm so afraid to drive like this, and there's no way I'm going back to that cabin."

From what she told me, it's almost an hour and a half to get where she is without traffic, and on a Friday afternoon at five o'clock, it'll be more like two if I'm lucky. Then again, I need some time to think about all this more clearly, to challenge every last detail of the plan. I've never in my life given serious thought to killing someone, but right now I'm feeling strongly about Dave being the first one to make the list. My initial thinking was to simply head up there and really kick the crap out of him - I mean, why wait for Tuesday? I'd take him out of action myself before he does any further damage. Who could fault me for that after what he did to her? But I don't think it's that simple anymore. The real problem is, he's gone ahead and brought a demented screwball like Ruben into the picture. And if I wind up beating Dave only half to death, I wonder if the problem will really go away, or if things might get even worse. What fate might await Vinny and Jill next time? And what about me?

"Where are you, exactly?" I grab a pad and pen from the counter. "Exit 16B off the thruway," I repeat it as I write it down, "the sign says Pineville, and you're at the Cartwheel Diner. Got it. Now if for any reason you have to move from there, make sure you use another pay phone to call me on my cell, okay?"

The last thing I need is my number showing up on her cell phone again, especially when Dave might be on the brink of having something real bad happen to him.

"I will," she agrees.

"Have you gone inside at all? Have many people seen you there?"

"No. I don't think anyone's really noticed me. The pay phone's out on the side of the building. Why?"

"Nothing. I just think we might be better off if it stays that way. Okay?"

"Okay. Whatever you say. I'll wait in my car."

"Good. I'll get there as fast as I can."

Hanging up the phone, I now sense his presence. How long he's been standing there I don't know. But what I do know is that he's not coming with me. This I have to do alone. I've already caused enough grief and anguish for him, and it's time for me to personally put an end to all of this nonsense. Mustering up my best game face, I turn towards him.

"Hey Chenz, I have to run out for a few minutes, can you keep an eye on the roast?"

"What's going on Michael?" He's got a solemn look on his face, but given the circumstances that doesn't necessarily mean anything.

"Ah, it's my Uncle Fred. Probably nothing too serious, but my aunt says he slipped on the kitchen floor again, she's having trouble getting him up by herself."

"Maybe I should go with you."

It sounded a bit challenging, and I'm sure he must have heard something, but maybe it wasn't all that much. Maybe he's not really sure and he's just feeling me out. Either way, I'm not caving in.

"No. Thanks. Just do me a favor and throw the potatoes in the top oven, it's all set to go. When the meat timer goes off, they'll both be ready. And *please*," I shift to a more reprimanding tone, "if for any reason I'm not back in time, don't wait for me, will you? You know how much it bothers me when people do that. You two get started without me, and I'll catch up. Okay?"

He begins to nod his head a little.

"Okay," he says evenly, still looking solemn as I head for the door.

I don't think I've ever lied to Vinny before in my life, and it feels terrible. But I'm sure if I told him the truth, he'd be the one leading the charge, and I can't let that happen. This score I need to settle by myself.

Chapter 44

I go over it again and again in my mind, and what really scares me is that I can't find anything wrong with it. I suppose that's why it impressed me so much when she first hit me with it. Not that I had given it any real consideration at the time, but I could tell it was a well thought out plan. I knew she had a sharp mind right from the start.

The amazing thing is, with the current circumstances being what they are, they only serve to make the whole idea even better.

I'll have to give him at least one hard shot to the face to knock him out and get him on the boat. But it's nothing inconsistent with the injuries he'll otherwise suffer from the accident. All I have to do then is make sure I wipe the boat down well. I have a couple of towels in the back of the truck for that. I'll also leave one of them on the shore to dry myself off with before I put my clothes back on.

Jill will follow me home, but stay at her house for the night. She'll call the cabin several times tomorrow morning - like a concerned wife might do after stranding her husband, even if he did abuse her.

I can picture her telling the police her tale of woe: *"Although he loses his temper and hits me once in awhile, I know he still really loves me, and I'm afraid something bad must have happened to him, because he always calls to apologize and make it up to me. But for some reason he didn't call me this time... And he was so drunk..."*

Who in their right mind would even consider the possibility that she went for a boat ride with him after what he did to her?

I leave the Bronx and the Major Deegan Expressway behind me, heading now for the start of the New York Thruway. Time-wise, I'm doing as well as I could have hoped for, especially in light of the fact that I used the cash lane at the bridge instead of my E-Z Pass. I don't think it would have been very wise to document where I'm going.

Chapter 45

It's an uncomplicated exit, with a small rectangular sign halfway up the ramp telling me to turn right for the Cartwheel Diner. After passing a single gas station and a small convenience store, the two-lane road curves to the left, and the diner comes into view just beyond the curve on the right. Closing in on it, I catch up to an eighteen-wheeler with his turning signal on, and I see several more of them idling on the near side of the parking lot. It must be one of those special eateries that the well traveled are partial to.

Clear of the entrance median, I slowly veer left of the semi, and I see her car off on the far side, just beyond the double row of cars parked near the building. I'm glad to see there aren't too many people coming and going, but a sufficient enough number that our meeting here shouldn't draw any particular attention. I pull alongside her Accord, the sight of the Tahoe startling her at first until she realizes it's me. I have the window down, so she can see me pointing to let her know I'm joining her, and to stay in the car.

I see the bruises on her face as soon as I slide into the passenger's seat, and I'm sure the rage I'm feeling is clearly visible in my expression.

She starts to cry. "I'm sorry I look so ugly."

Her arms wrap my neck and she buries her face against me. I feel her trembling.

"Stop it now. You don't look ugly," I lie, "and what are you sorry about? You did nothing wrong. You'll be fine in no time. I promise. Believe me, I'm about to take care of this guy, once and for all, so something like this will never happen again."

"Oh I don't know Michael. I'm not sure there's anything you can do to protect me from that animal. He's a lot crazier than I thought, and it sounds like some of his new friends are even worse."

"Yeah, I know... tell me... how's the boat running?"

"What?" She backs slightly away to look at me.

"The boat plan you told me about on the beach that night. I've been giving it some more thought. Maybe it's not such a bad idea."

"Really? I didn't think we would ever talk about that again. This all seems kind of sudden. Are you sure?"

"Well, with the way things are going, I'm thinking more and more that it might be the only viable option we have. That is, unless you tell me something has happened to change your mind."

"No, not at all. I guess I'm just surprised. And to be honest, I'm afraid to go back there and try to somehow sweet talk that evil pervert into a boat ride. I don't think I have the strength or the courage to do that right now."

"Don't worry, I'll do all the sweet talking."

Chapter 46

Dusk is approaching rapidly as we climb the narrow dirt and gravel road. A small cloud of dust flows up from underneath her car, and I'm trailing just far enough behind to keep it below my windshield. The first thing I better do when I get home, is hit this thing with a hose. I don't care what time it is. With my luck, it's probably some rare type of clay and soil that you can't find anywhere else on earth except here. Not that I suspect it matters all that much, but I'm not taking any unnecessary chances.

It's hard to believe I'm on my way to kill somebody. Premeditated murder is what they call this, the worst kind. But that's not the way it feels to me at all. It feels more like I'm on a mission of salvation to save someone I love, and that I'm fully justified in what I'm about to do. I've been very fortunate in my life, never having to fight a war. If I had, though, I imagine the rationale I would have used to keep my sanity would have been pretty much the same. You do these sort of horrible things when the alternative is even more deplorable. It's not that I haven't wrestled with a strong sense of guilt over this decision since I left the house, and God knows the closer I get the more I struggle. But all I have to do is think about what happened to Vinny, and then to Jill, and it gets real easy to recommit myself to what must be done.

This guy is a cancer and he has to be neutralized... permanently.

Of all the things to suddenly hit me, it occurs to me for the first time that I'm probably missing a beautiful sunset at the beach right now - on a Friday night no less. And that follows on the heels of spending a good part of last Friday night at The Clipper. I wouldn't have given very good odds of that happening at the start of the summer, that's for sure. Life does seem to take some interesting twists and turns when you least expect it. No regrets though. Once this nasty detail is out of the way, I'll start living the life I only dreamed of at the start of the summer.

Slowing down now, she pulls over slightly to the side and comes to a stop. I can't see the cabin yet, but she said it was just beyond the final bend in the road. I take a deep breath and open the door. It's show time.

As I approach her car, she gets out as well.

"I want to go with you."

"Jill, listen to me. I really don't want you to do that, and you already agreed you wouldn't."

"I know I did. But he can be so freaking treacherous, and you may need my help. I thought we were a team."

"Damn it! We are a team. But I can't be worried about your safety while I'm doing this. I'll call you just as soon as I knock him out, I promise I will. Don't forget, you have to help me get him to the boat, and I don't plan on dragging this out any longer than I have to."

"Okay," she's on the verge of crying again, "but just be careful, and don't give him a chance to pull anything dirty." She hugs me one last time.

"Trust me. I have no intentions of screwing this up."

I walk about a hundred feet to reach the bend, and even though the sun is below the trees as I round the corner, the majestic quality of the sight that awaits me is spectacular. A tiny cabin sits in the clearing almost directly in front of me, occupying only a small portion of the overall vista; most of it taken up by the huge lake sitting quietly beyond, surrounded by magnificent evergreens. I can't detect a single ripple in the water from this distance.

Too bad that's all about to change.

Getting closer to the cabin, I see the span of lawn that tapers down to the small finger dock, and the boat that waits there patiently to help me – so far, so good. I notice a dimly lit lantern aglow behind the only window on this side of the cabin, barely making a difference this early in the evening. If not for that, I'd swear this place was abandoned if I didn't know any better. Looking back one last time to make sure Jill isn't on my heels, all I can see is a bunch of grass, gravel, and tree trunks. I head for the point of no return, directly for the front door.

It hardly seems appropriate for me to knock, and I choose instead to turn the knob slowly, pressing slightly against the door to see if it's locked. It's not. I feel my pulse quicken as I push it further, hoping to increase my chances of surprise, but the squeal of old neglected hinges spoils everything.

"Is that you?" he growls loudly. "Where the hell have you been?"

He's standing there at the kitchen counter, leaning against his left hand, a bottle of Jack Daniels tilted up in the other... absorbed in the process of aiming it correctly at a glass of ice, not even looking this way.

Something about this scene is slightly disarming to me, but I can't for the life of me put a finger on what it is. The only thing I'm pretty sure of is that it has nothing to do with Dave and his present preoccupation.

Expecting a response that doesn't materialize, he finally looks over, swaying as he makes the turn, grabbing the edge of the countertop for help. My guess is there's a whole bunch of *woozy* going on inside of that large head of his. At least he'll never know what hit him.

"Hey!" he calls out, squinting to see me better, "aren't you that smart ass from the beach?" The words aren't close to flowing. "What in the hell are you doing in my house? Didn't your mother ever teach you how to knock?"

I hadn't planned on having a discussion, but as I get a sense for his sheer belligerence, I find myself wanting him to realize he's about to meet his maker, and why.

"Well, now that I know how much you like surprise parties, I thought I'd give you one of your own. I heard you had a lot of fun at the one you threw last night for my friend Vinny."

His head bobs back and forth with a smirk of arrogance, and the longer I watch it, the more I can't stand it.

"Are you out of your *fucking mind?*" he struggles to get the words out, "coming up here, barging in my house, talking in riddles."

"You know what Dave? I am out of my *fucking mind*, and you're the one that put me there. You think you're a tough guy slapping Jill around, don't you? So come on, why don't you try slapping me around?"

He puts the bottle down on the counter, and then raises the same hand to give me the finger.

"Why don't you kiss my big fat ass, and then get the hell out of my house before I call the cops."

So much for lengthy discussions - as far as I'm concerned, those were fitting enough final words from such a poor excuse of a human being. I walk straight up to him, my right fist cocked and ready to go. For some reason though, my eyes wander down to the bottles on the counter, and then it finally hits me. At first I'm telling myself to ignore it, it's too late in the game, and I'm sure there's a reasonable explanation that I don't have time for now. But I can't help myself, and I just have to ask.

"Who's drinking the rum?"

The bottle's close to empty, and I have this sick feeling starting to work its way into my stomach. I'm hoping to catch it in time.

"I said get out!"

I grab him forcefully by the collar, and give him one quick shot to the nose.

"And I asked you a question! Who's drinking the rum?"

Even in his inebriated state, the abrupt and painful assault clearly stuns and frightens him.

"It's none of your damn business!" he remains defiant, but the edge is gone from his voice. Fear now tempers his attitude.

Pulling him close to my face with my left hand, I make sure he notices my fist ready to strike once again.

"No. You see Dave, it is my damn business, and just maybe if you answer the question correctly, I won't have to *kill you*. At least not in the next few minutes."

Those words seem to get his attention. He's staring at me intently now.

"My wife was drinking it. What's the difference anyway?"

"No, no. I'll ask the questions. And while we're on a roll here, why don't you tell me why you slapped her around like you did?"

"What are you...?" he starts to ask, but then closes his eyes, looking as if he's trying to concentrate. Now he starts shaking his head up and down.

"Ahhhhh... now I get it." His head slumps down for a moment, then springs back somewhere close to center. "I'm a little slow... and very drunk at the moment... but I'm not stupid. I think I get it now. This whole trip was a setup... wasn't it? She brought you up here to kill me, didn't she?" I see tears welling up in his eyes. "You've been having an affair with her; like the one we had before Kevin was killed."

My stomach just took a severe turn for the worst, and for a split second, I think about going through with the murder just to shut him up, bring the situation to closure without question. *I get the girl, end of story*. But the thought of being potentially manipulated to this extent doesn't sit right with me at all, and the prize for committing such a serious crime, not quite as precious as it seemed when I first got here. The temptation passes quickly.

"Jill!" I yell as loudly as I can. "Come in here, will you?"

I'm not sure what I'm suffering more from, hurt or anger, but I have to know the truth about what's going on here before I go any further, and she's going to tell me. I ease up on my grip, but continue to watch him closely.

"You know Hubbard," the strange voice startles me, "I can't tell you how disappointing this is."

I turn quickly towards the open door, and there he is, taking up most of it.

"This was really quite simple... All you had to do was kill this guy, and we could have all lived happily ever after. You, me, and Jill, that is."

"Now isn't this special," Dave looks almost amused, "my beloved brother-in-law is in town for the gruesome ceremonies, just like last time."

"Why don't you shut your mouth David, before I have to shut it for you."

Dave looks like he's thinking about it.

"No, I have a better idea. Why don't you go *fuck yourself*, Ruben. You're going to kill me either way. The only thing of value I have left to my name is my life insurance, and that's what you're here for, isn't it?"

Ruben laughs. "You're right about that, partner. Two million bucks is nothing to sneeze at."

I'm speechless, looking back and forth at them, trying hard to process everything going down here. Shocked, angry, embarrassed, and afraid that I know too well what it is. It's all becoming surreal, and I feel my mind slipping into emotional overload.

"Jill is your sister?" I can't help the sound of surprise in my voice.

"Half sister. Same father," he says it as if that explains everything.

She appears at his side now, putting her arm around his waist, looking very business-like. His arm comes to rest on her shoulders. At least she's not smiling. How could she possibly come in here and face me like this, so cool and calm, after what she's done to me? I'm still so stunned, I can't even think of anything to say. I'm just staring at her.

"I'm sorry Michael."

"You're *sorry*?" I'm shaking my head in disbelief. "Why? Why me?"

"Oh... that was my idea," Ruben answers. "I mean, there we were, in need of a patsy; and then it occurred to me that I had never gotten around to settling the score with you and your buddy D'Angelo over that little incident we had back in high school. It seemed like such a nice fit. You didn't think I had forgotten about that, did you? By the way, how is my old pal doing? I sure hope he isn't still sore at me about last night." He laughs harder now than before.

I have to get a handle on myself, and figure out what I'm going to do. The gun he has stuck in his pants is all too obvious, and odds are, even without the gun, he could easily beat the crap out of me.

"So, here's the deal," he focuses back on me as he says it. "When you first came in here, it didn't really matter much to me whether you killed him or just beat him senseless. I would have finished him off if you didn't, and pinned the murder on you either way. Believe it or not, though, my sister here has grown kind of fond of you, and she was sort of hoping for the boat ride thing. That way, the two of you could have gotten married in a year or so - and of course in the mean time, continued to enjoy each other's company, if you catch my drift. And I could have started helping you and D'Angelo run your business. You know, just like I did with old Dave here."

"It's not too late for that Michael," she actually sounds serious.

The thought of that scenario flashes through my mind, and I find it so repulsive I couldn't possibly even describe it. The idea of selling out my dear friend Vinny, having these two use me at will, sucking every last dime out of my pocket, and every last ounce of dignity from my soul, the same as they did to Dave. I look at him standing there, ready to accept his fate - a worn out, beaten man. I can't help but wonder what he was like before he ran into these two. I feel so ashamed I unwittingly helped the process.

"So what do you say, Hubbard? Think you might still want to give it a shot? I can assure you one thing, it'll be much less painful for you than plan B."

He makes it sound like we're conducting a routine business meeting here, and I'm sure to him, that's all it is.

What I'm finding much harder to deal with is that Jill's standing there shaking her head up and down ever so slightly, with a friendly expression that urges me to accept the offer. Like I'm supposed to believe, after everything that's happened, she's making some kind of a heartfelt connection with me.

"*What do I say…?*" I know I should probably be a little careful here, in spite of how I really feel, but the emotional side of me is screaming for attention, and I can't seem to keep it sufficiently tempered. "I say the two of you belong in a *fucking loony bin*. One with really thick rubber walls."

Dave gets a laugh out of hearing me say that, and even though it was unintended, I suddenly feel a little bit better about myself, giving him some small amount of pleasure in his final hour.

"Have it your way," Ruben hardly seems to care. "I tried to tell you not to waste your time sis."

"But it won't be so easy to collect the two million bucks without my help, will it?" I try to keep the conversation going as long as I can.

"Au contraire, old friend, it's very easy. It's called a murder-suicide." He reaches for the pistol. "You see, this gun here is one of Dave's... I took the liberty of borrowing it; I didn't think he'd mind... And the way this tragic scene unfolds, is that he first shoots his wife's lover, *which would be you*, and then, totally grief stricken, he turns it on himself... It happens all the time."

Now I'm scared to death, and probably not far from it. Maybe I should experience a sudden change of heart and try to buy us more time.

"Can anybody in there help me?" The voice calls from somewhere outside. "I'm looking for a *pussy* by the name of *Sanchez!* You in there Ruben?"

I should have known: no argument to speak of after giving him that lame excuse, and no attempts to reach me on my cell. He followed me... But this is exactly why I didn't want him to do that.

"What a nice surprise," Ruben's licking his chops, "I guess I'm in the bonus round. Now we get to have a triple murder, and I couldn't imagine a more deserving threesome."

He backs up to the open door.

"Yeah! I'm here D'Angelo! Ready to kick your fucking ass again, just like I did last night! Come on in if you think you're man enough!"

I notice darkness has arrived, and I'm sure Ruben can't see much of anything out there; but I also know the lighting in here is so dim, that almost the same holds true for Vinny.

"Watch it Vinny! He's got a gun!"

Ruben turns in the doorway to face me, the gun now free from his waist.

"You know Hubbard, I had to shoot your sorry ass sooner or later anyway, so why not do it now."

The piercing sound of an engine racing at full throttle gets his attention, and then I hear it being dropped into gear, gravel now spitting wildly from a wheel fighting for traction. The noise becomes thunderous as it bears down on the cabin, and the gun comes up quickly, firing a few shots into the night. Before I ever hear the fourth round leave the barrel, a deafening crash rocks the cabin, but not before Ruben's body took the initial blow. It was a vicious crunch of solid metal meeting human flesh and bone, launching him back through the door, and completely across the room. Hitting the far wall on the fly, he collapses instantly to the floor. I think it's a safe bet he's dead.

"Ruben! Oh Ruben!" Jill is now hysterical.

I grab the gun before she decides to use it next, and then turn for the door, worried sick that Vinny took a bullet for me. What awaits me there is something to behold.

I feel a rush of relief and a smile coming to my face as the sight unfolds before me. The twisted grill of the vehicle fills the entire door, with steam hissing from a busted radiator, rising up and around the words that are painted backwards across the front of the hood: *Carbone Brothers*. And there they are, sitting side by side, both of their thumbs pumped up in the air, big smiles on their faces. It's not too hard to tell that Frank has the wheel. I also see a bullet hole through the middle of the windshield. Thank God it didn't hit one of them.

"You know Michael…" It's Vinny, coming into the tiny room from the rear of the house. "If you plan on ever lying to me again…"

"Don't worry Chenz, it'll never happen." I meet him with my arms open, and we hold each other tightly in a bear hug.

"Yeah… but if you do," he backs away enough to palm my cheek, "I suggest you get a lot of practice in between now and then. Because, in case nobody ever told you this before, you are one hell of a lousy liar… Although, if you had told me the truth this time, we might both be dead right now."

"I suppose you're right about that."

Only Vinny can find the good in whatever I do.

"Vinny!" Here come the twins, up and over the steaming hood.

"What do you think buddy?" Frank asks. "Pretty good hit huh?"

"Hey! You two crazy bastards really came through tonight, that's for sure."

Vinny fakes a couple of jabs at Frank's stomach, then grabs them both around their shoulders, pulling them in close. They look like they just took top prize on a game show.

"Hey Michael!" Joe has his hand out, "good to see you man. Glad we could help you out."

I shake both their hands.

"There's no way I could ever thank you guys enough for what you did tonight." I know it comes out sounding a bit mushy, but I really couldn't care less.

"Hey! Don't mention it," Frank keeps it on the light side, "that's what friends are for."

Smiling at the two of them, I shake my head in agreement. A man could do much worse than having these two as friends, and from now on I'll be making sure I don't forget that.

I notice Dave bending over Jill, trying his best to console her. My guess is, in spite of everything that's happened, he really loves her.

"Would you guys excuse me for a minute, I need to talk to them."

"Yeah," Vinny says, "I'll give the cops a shout, and we probably need a tow truck for the van."

Stepping towards them, I get a close up view of Ruben for the first time, and it doesn't look good at all. Jill's up on her feet though, and from all appearances, she's already shifted back to her business mode, trying her best to size up the mess and figure out what she might be able to do to minimize the damage to herself. I guess Ruben must have taught her well, or maybe it was the other way around.

"Michael, you have to know..."

"No! I don't have to know anything more than I already do... Dave, I'm sorry."

"You don't have to..."

"Yes I do. What I did was very, very wrong, and I am sorry. I had an affair with your wife, and I almost killed you."

Glancing at Jill, I think of how badly she used me, and how much I'd love to wring her neck right now. But the sympathy I'm feeling for Dave far outweighs my scorn for her.

"Now when the cops arrive, I plan on telling them the truth about coming here with the intent to beat you, but nothing more than that. That is, unless one of you want to take the story in that direction, and then I'll be happy to. It might be easier on the both of you, though, if we let Ruben be the fall guy... I don't know what your lives were like before I came into the picture, and I'm sure I don't want to know the truth about what happened to Kevin. All I really want to do, is to forget I ever met either one of you. Understand?"

"Michael, I never meant to..."

"*Jill*. Do me a big favor, and put a lid on the bullshit. I've already heard enough to last me a lifetime. You have some serious problems right now, and if I were you, I'd use the time before the cops get here to take stock of myself, and then I'd be huddling with Dave, trying to figure out how I wanted to spend the rest of my life. Maybe if you try real hard, you might even come up with something better than being a trophy wife for some nasty looking dyke in prison. But at this point, I honestly don't care what you do. I'm just trying to give you an option, hoping like hell that somewhere deep down inside, there's some degree of goodness in you."

I see the wheels turning, and I think she finally understands that the gig is up and over. She nods at me with a solemn look, and then turns to Dave, starting to cry. He wraps an arm around her shoulder, and she grabs a hold of his waist. God only knows how sincere those tears might be, but after what I almost did tonight, far be it from me to judge anyone.

Dave extends his free hand; he's still three sheets to the wind, but trying hard to bring himself around. "Thanks. I appreciate this."

I shake it without saying another word, and then take my leave.

Chapter 47

It's been almost two weeks since I made that trip to the cabin, and I still can't believe how quickly I let my life get so far out of hand. I had always thought of myself as a pretty savvy guy, plenty of street smarts, able to smell a hustle a mile away. And yet there I was, being played like a fiddle, completely enthralled by the beauty and sexual favors of a woman, ready to commit murder no less, based on little more than hearsay from someone I hardly knew at all. No matter how you look at it, pretty shameful stuff to be a part of.

I'm not much of a religious man, but I do believe there is a God; and just in case he had anything to do with giving me a second chance, I went ahead and thanked him more times than I can count this week. As far as the embarrassment goes, I know from experience that there's no substitute for time when you're trying to heal from that feeling.

But I know something else too, better now than I ever have before in my life: True love and honest friendship is a rare and precious thing, and if you're fortunate enough to experience it, remember to embrace it and cherish it often. Most people aren't lucky enough to ever get the chance.

Chapter 48

I'm getting a little worried about Vinny. He's been with April every night since she first brought him to my house. And even though he's not one to normally indulge the "L" word, he's used it on more than one occasion to describe certain things about her, like the way she dresses, and the way she smiles. He's even said he loves her cooking, and I don't remember him ever saying that about any woman other than his mother.

He's sitting across from me right now, on the opposite side of my desk. We're waiting on a phone call from Fat Tony; evidently he's in desperate need of the parts we made, but having trouble coming up with the cash. What a surprise.

"Every time I look at her, I can't help but think about how she stayed up all night and watched over me. Taking care of me."

I can't believe I'm hearing this. "I thought even thinking about that kind of stuff made you miserable, you know... *some woman doting all over you*. I thought you and I already had each other for that sort of nonsense."

"*We do* Michael. But you have to understand, *this* is different."

"Oh, really? *I* have to understand?"

"Yeah... Sometimes, I'm just watching her do something, anything at all, and all of a sudden I get this strange sort of feeling in my gut... Not a bad feeling, just strange; a *good* strange. I'm not sure how else to describe it."

He's sitting there looking serious, apparently satisfied with his explanation. Then his face suddenly breaks into one of those full-blown goofy looking smiles. I can't help myself, and I burst out laughing.

"What's so damn funny?" he looks genuinely upset. "I'm trying to tell you something here."

"You're funny, that's what."

"And why is that?"

"Because I think you finally found your match."

"What do you mean, my match?"

"You are *in love*, my friend."

"Give me a break, will you? I was trying to have a serious conversation."

I start laughing again, and after a few seconds his smile returns.

"You think that might be what it is, huh? Well, to tell you the truth, I was starting to wonder myself. It's really some kind of a feeling."

"Yes it is."

I'm still chuckling, nodding my head up and down when the phone rings.

"Michael Hubbard." I leave it on the speaker.

"Hey Michael, Tony here. Listen to me. I've helped you out a lot in the past, and right now I really need *you* to help *me*. Understand?"

This guy's got some set of balls.

"No! Tony! I don't understand. So stop right there. Before you insult my intelligence again, let's get something straight. Any business we've ever conducted has benefited you every bit as much as it has me, if not more. You wouldn't have done it otherwise. So don't you *dare* ever say that to me again. Do *you* understand?"

He clears his throat. "Okay, okay. I'm sorry I said it that way. But these freaking twins really have me by the short hairs, and I don't have enough cash to go around. I've got important customers crawling up my ass looking for parts I don't have, and I'm in serious trouble here."

I smile at the thought of Frank and Joe, and what his recent conversations with those two must be like.

"Let me ask you something, Tony. Do you have any equity at all? I mean, hard assets that aren't already encumbered as collateral on some other loan. And please don't lie to me when you answer, because if you say you do, I'll want to legally secure something tangible before you ever touch the parts."

"Well, yeah. I still own my house. But that's the only safety cushion that I have."

"So then you have a decision to make Tony... And what I'll do for you is this: if the house is in fact free and clear of any liens like you say, I'll accept it as collateral against an interest free loan for two years. But make no mistake about it, if you don't pay me by then, I'm taking the house."

"You'd do that for me?"

"With only two conditions."

"And what might they be?"

"The first one is - you pay the twins whatever you owe them."

"Okay. I have no choice anyway. Those pricks aren't budging. And two?"

"You come over here next Wednesday for Employee Appreciation Day, and you help Vinny and I serve lunch to everyone."

"What?"

"Yeah. You put on an apron, you help barbecue some burgers and dogs, and most importantly, you smile like you really mean it, and thank my people for the fabulous work they do for you."

"What in the hell are you trying to do, totally embarrass me?"

"Not at all, maybe just humble you a little. And you never know, you might even get a kick out of seeing how much they appreciate you doing that for them."

"I don't know... I think I'd rather pay interest. How long are we talking about?"

"No more than an hour, I promise. And I'll tell you what - we'll be more than happy to come over to your place and do the same for you. You'd be surprised how well people respond to that kind of thing."

"All right... let's not get too carried away here. What time do you want me there?"

Chapter 49

"Now *Chenz*, you're sure you're okay with this, right? A good chunk of this change is yours too, and we might not be seeing it for awhile."

"Absolutely. I think it's a good thing you're doing, helping the twins get their money."

"After what they did for me, it's the least I could do. How are they making out with the boat search?"

"They're having a survey done tomorrow on that twenty-six foot Sea Ray I told you about."

"That's good. Did you tell them about docking it at my house?"

"Yeah. They couldn't believe it. I think you really touched them with that one."

"I'm glad… Hopefully, they won't get into too much trouble with that thing, although, the thought of those two behind the wheel of any sizable boat is pretty scary. Did you happen to mention there's a functional reason for those red and green buoys scattered all over the bay?"

He smiles. "Yeah. They thought I was joking at first."

"Well, God knows we'll be having moments of severe regret with those two around most of the time, but I figure we'll somehow manage through it all."

"I'm sure we will... Hey, are you bringing the boat over tonight?"

"Yeah, right after my dinner date."

"Dinner date? Who's the lucky girl?"

"Sorry old friend, but after that last fiasco, I'm afraid to even tell you her name until I see how things go tonight. But if all goes even half as well as I'm hoping it will, you might be seeing her at the beach this weekend."

Chapter 50

I enter through the front door, passing the bar on my way to the dining room, waving to a few regulars as I go. Just shy of seven o'clock, it's already packed, but I made a reservation this time, not taking any chances at this hour.

Happy that I got here first, I catch Kathy's attention and point to the table I'm almost certain is mine. Getting the nod I was looking for, I take the seat that backs me up against the corner. This works nicely.

She finishes pouring some coffee at a nearby table, and then takes my order for a glass of cabernet. It'll be dark by the time I bring the boat over tonight, and I'll be better off if I stay away from the hard stuff. Not that I couldn't use a strong belt of scotch right now to calm me down a little, but I'm sure I'll be fine once we get past the initial hello.

Here she comes now, through the side entrance, wearing a very sexy summer dress. It's light rose in color, more like a soft pastel, and it has the tiniest little shoulder straps holding the top in place. It seems to hug her upper curves and slender stomach so gently as she moves, and the length of it below her waist sort of flutters with the stride of those great looking legs. The only thing more noticeable than the sparkle of her diamond necklace and the matching earrings is the warmth of her wonderful smile.

I get up to kiss her hello, "You look absolutely stunning."

"You don't look so bad yourself."

I hold the chair until she sits. "Chardonnay?"

"That would be nice Michael, thank you."

No sooner do I take my seat, than I see him honing in on us. It looks like he's making a beeline this time.

"Michael! How are you sir?" He winks his approval.

"Pretty good Ned. How about you? You look thirsty."

"Parched."

He turns, all smiles, holding his hand out to take hers.

"I must say Gina, you certainly look ravishing tonight. It's been a long time since I've seen Michael with someone so beautiful."

"Why thank you Ned," she smiles, blushing slightly, "how nice of you to say that."

He's such a charmer.

I'm tempted for a second to stick my arm between them to wave Kathy over, but it's much more fun to watch the both of them enjoy the moment without interruption.

*

"It was quite a surprise, hearing from you again, though certainly a wonderful one. May I ask what brought about the sudden change of heart?"

"Well... I suppose it was a combination of things really. You might say I've recently gained a much greater appreciation for how precious a second chance can be... But even more important than that, regardless of what happened between us in the past, I'm still hopelessly in love with you. I always have been, and I can't imagine that ever changing."

Her hands softly cover the both of mine resting flat against the table.

"I love you too Michael, so much more than I realized when I started to stray, and I'm sorry beyond words for the way I hurt you. Just wait and see how much I prove it to you this time."